HER WAGON TRAIN
PINKERTON

LONDON JAMES

long
VALLEY
PRESS

OREGON TRAIL BRIDES

Four orphans and their headmistress set out for Oregon in search of men looking for mail-order brides. Will they find what they are looking for? Or will fate have other plans?

SERIES RELEASES STARTING IN EARLY 2023

ONE

CHARLOTTE

*C*hildren don't expect their world to change in an instant. They haven't lived through the horrors that adults have, not knowing about love, loss, pain, and heartbreak. They only see the fun in life. The happy. They live in a world without monsters—well, perhaps they believe in fake ones, but not the real ones. Not the ones that are lurking around every corner. The ones that wish to steal away all the happiness. The ones who let the devil whisper in their ears, telling them lies upon lies until their minds are so twisted that they believe they can do and take anything they want just because they want it.

It's not until they witness it as a child or grow up that people see the truth behind the world. That it's not a friendly place. That evil waits around every turn. That horror can change your life in an instant. And that there is no rest from the devil nipping at your heels.

*T*he autumn air was crisp with the hints of fall, and while Charlotte sat on a bench with her face buried in a heaping pile of cotton candy, other fairgoers meandered around the town's county fair. Charlotte had been looking forward to the festival for a month. "It will be the event of the town," her father had said about it that morning as they left the house.

She had dreamed of balloons, cotton candy, candied apples, and handfuls of popcorn for weeks until the morning of the fair arrived. It had been the one thing she'd looked forward to since her Mama passed, and while she wished her mama was there, she also didn't want any sorrow to get her down.

Not today.

Not at the fair.

She kicked her legs as she sat on the bench, biting at the pile of sugary string that melted on her tongue before she even had a chance to chew. She could feel it stick to the sides of her cheeks, but she didn't care. It was only more sugary goodness that she would be able to lick off when she was finished.

"Excuse me, little girl," a voice asked her.

Charlotte looked up toward a couple looking down at her. The woman smiled while the man furrowed his brow.

"Are you lost?" the woman asked.

Charlotte shook her head, letting her tiny Irish accent purr. "I'm here with my Pa."

"Oh." The woman brushed her fingers against her chest. "I'm sorry, but you are sitting here alone. We just thought we would help in case you were lost."

"Thank yeh, but I'm not."

The husband and wife seemed to accept Charlotte's answer, and they walked off, letting her happily get back to the delicious pink cloud of sugar in her hand, and she continued to kick her feet, swinging them back and forth. The white lace on her dress swished from her movement. It had been a special dress her Pa had brought home just for the fair.

"A special girl and a special occasion need an extra special dress," he had said, handing her the box.

She opened it as though it was a present at Christmas, ripping at the bow so fast she untied it in seconds before she shoved the top of the box off and brushed the tissue paper away from the dress. She didn't want to tell her father how the bright white color scared her a little as she knew she would spend the entire day worrying over not getting it dirty, but she also knew that no matter the worry, she loved it anyway.

It made her feel beautiful even before she tried it on.

Minutes ticked by as Charlotte continued to finish off her cotton candy. It wasn't until she ate the last bite, licked her fingers clean, and wiped her face that she bothered to look around. People continued meandering in all different directions. While most ignored the little girl sitting on the bench alone, some looked at her as they passed. A few whispered and pointed, and after another couple approached her, asking if she was lost, she finally got off the bench and began wandering around the booths and tents, looking for her Pa. Of course, he had told her to stay put and that he'd return. Still, he'd also said he would come back before she finished.

And he wasn't back yet.

She furrowed her brow as she continued through the crowd, and the men, women, and children enjoyed the fair around her. The sounds and commotion distracted her, and she rounded a booth, heading down a small space between several tents. Kind of like a back alley; there was no one around her. At least not until she rounded the corner and found her Pa talking to another man.

"I don't care what you say, Mr. McLaren. I don't have your money." The man waved his hands.

"Oh, yeh are gonna care, Mr. Carter. Because if I don't get me money, there will be hell to pay." Her pa pointed his finger at the man's chest, and the two moved closer together.

Charlotte froze and sucked in a breath. She glanced over at several crates stacked behind one of the tents and lunged for them, hiding behind them as she crouched down and peeked through the slots between the wood.

"Oh, is that so?" Mr. Carter backed away from her pa. "And what are you going to do about it?"

Her pa stepped toward the man again. "I don't think yeh want to know what I'm gonna do about it."

"Well, I'll have to call your bluff on that." The man stepped back a few more steps and dug his hand into his jacket pocket. He yanked out a gun and pointed it toward her pa.

Charlotte gasped and slapped her hand over her mouth. She wanted to run to her pa, but no matter how much she willed her feet to move, they didn't.

Her pa raised his hands. "Don't be pointing that thing at me, thinking yeh can push me around."

"I don't think I can push you around. I know I can."

"Yeh owe me that money fair and square. I got bills to pay, Mr. Carter. I have a daughter to care for."

"You think I care about that?" Mr. Carter waved the gun, relaxing his stance.

Her pa lunged for him, and the two men struggled. Charlotte ran out from behind the crates. "Pa!" she screamed.

Her pa's head whipped toward her. "Get out of here, Charlotte."

As she spun, the gun went off, and the gunshot echoed between the tents. She turned around as her father fell to the ground, and Mr. Carter ran from the alleyway.

"Pa!" Charlotte shouted again as she ran for her pa. She fell to her knees beside him. Tears welled in her eyes as he lay on the ground, struggling to breathe.

He gasped and looked at her. "Charlotte."

"I'm going to get help." She tried to stand, but he reached out and stopped her.

"No."

"But you need help." Her tears broke free from her eyes and streamed down her cheeks. They smelled of the sugar she had missed while trying to clean her face of the cotton candy.

"There's nothing . . . nothing you can do. I love yeh, Charlotte. Yeh *will always be my little lass. Always."* He took a few more breaths and then he was gone.

*C*harlotte's eyes opened, and she looked up at the Idaho sky. The sun had yet to peek over the horizon, but the darkness of night had already begun to fade into a dull gray. It was a beautiful morning wrecked by the nightmare that replayed in her mind more times than she cared to admit. Her pa's death and how a man named Mr. Carter murdered him, taking everything away from her all in a matter of a few seconds.

She rolled over, looking at the campfire burning in the stone pit. The once large flames had died, leaving a charred log in the middle. Burnt black, it glowed orange in several places. She sat up, letting the blanket fall to the ground as she moved her legs out from under it and slid her boots on before standing.

Her shoulders and back ached as she stretched, and she yawned. Every inch of her was tired, and even her tired was tired, if that made sense. With only a few hundred more miles to their journey, they had been traveling for nearly six months. Perhaps even longer than that. She'd lost count of the days months ago.

She made her way over to the fire, bending down to grab more kindling, and as she threw it on and stoked the little flame that remained, it hit the kindling, growing again.

"Bad dream?" a voice asked behind her.

She flinched, then turned to find Uncle Ned stumbling toward her. He rubbed his eyes and blinked as though he'd just woken up.

"Did I wake yeh?" she asked, a slight hint of remorse whispered through her tone. She hadn't meant to wake him up.

"Nah." He waved his hand and then stretched his back. "I rolled over onto a rock. Lord, I can't wait until we are in

Oregon, and I can enjoy a bed again. Roughing it on the ground is not for me." He yawned and sat down on the log by the fire.

"Well, we should be there soon, so . . ." She let her voice trail off as she grabbed the kettle and started the coffee, hanging it over the fire.

"Yeh didn't say what woke yeh up. Did yeh roll over on a rock too?" he asked.

"Something like that."

Uncle Ned heaved a deep sigh, shaking his head. "Yeh know there was nothing yeh could do, Lass." His Irish accent always got deeper the lower his voice was, reminding Charlotte of her pa.

"I know," she lied.

Of course, at five years old, there hadn't been anything she could have done, really. She knew that. But she still felt as though she could have done something. If she'd run off to find Ned when she first saw her father arguing, perhaps he'd still be alive. Instead, she hid behind the crates, watching and doing nothing.

He looked at her as though he knew she was lying but didn't press the matter again. "I've been thinking about what we're gonna do when we get to Oregon. What do yeh say to a lumber mill?"

"But won't they have those?"

He waved his hand again. "Aye, probably, but that doesn't mean they don't need more. Certainly, there will always be a need, and yeh know the Irish are great for making deals." He winked, and she smiled.

"Especially, yeh, Uncle Ned."

He winked again and pointed at her, making a clicking sound with his tongue. "And don't yeh forget it, Lass." They laughed, and as they settled, his smile vanished. "So, lumber mill. What do yeh think?"

"I think it will be great."

"For us?"

"For yeh? Yes. For me? I don't know."

He heaved another deep sigh, growling under his breath. "Don't tell me yeh are still wasting yer breath on that silly notion of finding that man and getting yer revenge."

"It's not a silly notion."

"Yeah, it is. And the sooner yeh realize it, Lass, the better." Another growl vibrated through his chest. "Doing away with that man isn't gonna bring yer pa home."

"I know it's not."

"Then why go after him? Why not just live yer life, making it as happy as yeh can? That's what yer pa would want, and yeh know I'm right."

She opened her mouth to argue but couldn't think of anything to say. She didn't want to admit that her uncle was right. She knew her pa wouldn't want her wasting away her life following the man who killed him. Yet knowing this didn't change the fact that such is all that she wanted to do. No one understood why she needed to do what she did, but that didn't mean the idea didn't hold validity.

At least, she thought so.

"Yeh need to forget this man—"

"He has a name. Mr. Jack Carter."

"Whatever yeh want to call him, I don't care. Yeh need to forget about him. Let it go. Just live yer life." Uncle Ned pointed toward the other wagons in the camp. "All yer friends, Abby, Emma, Lillian, and even Sadie . . . they are all married and starting families. Yeh should do that too."

Charlotte looked around at the wagons while everyone was still sleeping, and as she looked at each bonnet, she thought of the friends she'd shared so much with on this journey. Of course, she hadn't spoken to them much lately. With Sadie gone, a piece of her felt gone, and there was a disconnection between her and the other three. It was as though she was an outsider all over again, and she missed Sadie even more than she ever did.

"I don't think I want that life, Uncle Ned. I'm not like them."

He tucked his chin down, nodding slightly as he inhaled a deep breath. "Will yeh at least promise me yeh will think about it?"

"Yes, Uncle Ned. I will," she lied again.

TWO

NICOLAS

*F*ort Boise.

And the bane of Nicolas's existence.

It was just another fort with just another commanding officer who seemed more interested in helping his own needs than another—especially a Pinkerton like Nicolas.

At least, that was how Nicolas felt as he sat at the commanding officer's desk, listening to the man go on and on about how much he's done for this outpost since he got assigned here. If Nicolas heard 'it was deplorable when I arrived, but I turned it around one more time, he knew he would go crazy.

"So, that's when I told him I wouldn't leave my post unless I had orders from the general himself." The commander pointed his finger toward his desk, tapping the wood with several hard taps that made the skin on his fingertips turn white. "If I leave here, I guarantee this place will return to the lawless wasteland it was before I got here." The officer leaned back in his chair and kicked his feet onto the desk, crossing them at the ankles. "Did you want another glass of water?" he asked.

Nicolas glanced down at the still-full glass in front of him.

He hadn't touched it since the officer's right-hand man set it in front of him nearly an hour ago. His brow furrowed, and he shook his head. He didn't have time for this nonsense. He had a man to catch. He had a murderer to catch. "No, thank you," he said flatly.

The officer eyed him for a moment, then sat up, resting his forearms on the desk. "So, what can I do for you today, Mr. Kelly?"

"Well, it's like I said when I asked for a meeting, I'm looking for this man." Nicolas looked down at the wanted picture in front of him and then touched it, pushing it toward the officer. "His name is Jack Carter, and he's wanted in three states for six different murders. Or I suppose six that we know of. There could be more."

"And what makes you think you'll find him here?"

"There are several Pinkertons who are tracking him, and one of them believed him to be in this area."

"So, what is it you want me to do?"

Nicolas fought a groan under his breath, and although he wanted to roll his eyes, he didn't. He'd already told the man what he needed. Twice. Officer Mills was just another typical Commanding Officer, just like everyone Nicolas knew. One who talks of power and his stance and position in the United States military, yet never does anything of importance. He often even hides behind his men, letting them do all the dirty work he wouldn't do.

Lord, how Nicolas loathed Officers of the Cavalry.

"You know what? Never mind. I'll take care of it." He leaned forward and snatched the picture from the desk as he stood. He folded the paper and shoved it into his jacket pocket. "If you will at least do me the favor of letting me ask around some of your men to see if any of them have seen Mr. Carter, I would be grateful."

"Of course. Ask them anything you like."

Nicolas tipped his hat and then made his way to the door, not even pausing before he left the commander's office.

Sunlight beat down on his back, causing a thin layer of sweat to slick the back of his neck. He glanced around the fort, watching the people meandering through the supply tents. So many folks stopped to buy the last things they would need before making the final stretch to Oregon. He searched through the faces, but none was the one he was looking for.

He trotted down the steps, making his way through the crowd. While most men, women, and children moved out of his way after noticing the silver badge on his chest, there were a few men who seemed to notice it and closed in on him as though they were trying to intimidate him.

He'd seen it countless times; men thought they were more powerful or had the upper hand because there was only one of him and more of them. It was a foolish notion that all, so far in Nicolas's five years he'd had the badge, had come to regret. It almost amused him now, watching them think they could push him around.

He spied a group of soldiers near a few of the tents and made his way toward them, reaching into his jacket pocket and yanking out the wanted picture once more.

"Good afternoon, men," he said to them.

They each nodded, muttering their own versions of a greeting, whether it was a good afternoon, a hello, or even what Nicolas thought was a greeting in Spanish.

"Have you seen this man?" he asked them.

They all looked down at the paper and shook their heads. Of course, he'd known this wouldn't be easy. Tracking down any man was never anything else other than hard, but still, with each shake of someone's head when asked if they'd seen a man, the struggle of finding the one he looked for became even more annoying.

He didn't like searching for someone.

He only liked finding them.

After thanking the soldiers, he continued on, asking a few more if they'd seen the man in the picture. Each time he was met with nothing but no until finally, as the afternoon gave way to the early evening, his stomach growled with hunger, and he stopped in the tent serving hot meals.

"What will it be, Sir?" a man asked as he entered the tent. He glanced around at the tables, looking through the faces. Most of the other men and women ignored him, but some eyed him for a moment before dropping their gazes to the ground.

"What do you have?" he asked the cook.

"I got some hot chili and cornbread for a quarter."

Nicolas handed him two quarters, dropping them in the man's palm. "I'll take two."

"Coming right up, Sir."

Nicholas continued glancing around the tent while the man shuffled around, pouring two spoonfuls of chili into two bowls, cutting off two chunks of cornbread, and setting them on a plate. Before the man turned back toward him, he yanked out the paper. "Have you seen this man?" he asked the cook.

"No, Sir. I haven't." He handed over the food. "But I got to admit I don't have much for memory anymore. Not like I used to when I was young. I also see so many men. Even if I had seen him, I doubt I would remember."

"Thank you for your honesty." Nicolas took the bowls and plate and made his way back outside, sitting at a table near the tent as he tried to ignore a table of four men sitting not too far from him, staring.

"Rhett?" one of them said to the other one. "Hey, Rhett? Rhett?"

"What?" Another one—presumably, Rhett—whipped his head around to the other. "Can't you see I'm busy?"

"Busy doing what?" the first asked.

"None of your business."

The other two at the table sat quietly, watching the back-and-forth banter between the two talking.

"So, Rhett, what are we doing today? Are we gonna leave like you said we was?"

"I don't know. Part of me thinks we should hang around the fort for a little longer."

"How much longer?"

"Until we find us a job on a wagon train. Surely there will be one who comes through here needing some cowboys."

"Why don't we go to Oregon as we planned? Why do we need to find work?"

Rhett turned to the first man and slapped him on the back of the head. "Because I told you already we need money for supplies. I swear you are nothing but a fool. I don't know why I agreed to let you come with us."

The two watching the others laughed, and the first man rubbed the back of his head, casting Rhett a sour glare.

Nicolas snorted at the scene, and he watched from the corner of his eye as he dug his spoon into the chili and took a big bite. Much too bland for his taste, he grimaced.

"Would you look at who is approaching the tent, boys," Rhett said, slapping his hand on the table.

Nicolas moved his eyes without moving his head, noticing a mother and two older daughters walking toward them. A groan vibrated through his chest at the scene unfolding in his mind.

They better not harass the three women, he thought. Noticing how the four of them all straightened up in their seats, his stomach clenched at the trouble brewing.

"Well, howdy, ladies," Rhett said as the women neared the table. "May I invite you to join us?"

The two daughters looked at their mother and giggled while the mother glared at the four men. "Not today," she said.

"Aw, come on. We could order another round of chili, and I can send Billy here for a round of whiskey from the next tent.

We could have ourselves a great time getting to know each other."

"There's nothing I want to know about you that I don't already know. You and your men need to leave my daughters and me alone."

Rhett's smile faded. "Well, now that's just rude. We could be fine gentlemen, ma'am, and you just judged us without knowing us. You don't know us. We could make fine husbands for your daughters."

"I don't want to get married," one of the others who had been silent up until now said.

"All right. I stand corrected." Rhett looked at his men and then at the mother. "Two of the three of us could be fine husbands for your daughters."

The two young women giggled again, and the mother whipped her head toward them. "Hush. You girls want nothing to do with these men. I assure you. Not to mention your father will forbid it. They are nothing but vagrants. They have nothing to their names, no money, no land."

"How do you know we got no money or land?" Rhett stood, and the force of his movement shoved his chair backward.

Nicolas's chest tightened. He hadn't signed up for this today.

"Are you saying you have it then?" The woman asked. She folded her arms across her chest. "Because your clothes say otherwise."

"Again, with the assumptions." Rhett moved around to the other side of the table, pointing his finger at the woman.

Nicolas took another bite of his chili, watching the men.

The three women backed away, and the daughters looked at their mother while the mother clutched her chest.

"Get away from us," she said. Her voice cracked.

"Or else what?"

Nicolas took a third bite, chewing and swallowing before he

said. "Why don't you just do us all a favor and do as the lady asked."

He glanced down at the chili, collecting another bite of it in his spoon. He could see the four men turn toward him out of the corner of his eye.

"And just what business of it is yours, old man?" Rhett asked.

There were a few times in Nicolas's life when words irked him. One of them was when another man asked him if something was his business—especially when it clearly was and when someone thought of him as an older gentleman. He wasn't much older than the four of them, but for some reason, no matter where he went, others always assumed he was older.

"I think it is every man's business when another man bothers a lady. Or, in this case, three ladies." He took another bite of chili, glancing down at the bowl as he moved slowly.

"Well, I don't."

"Maybe that's your problem then."

"Teach him a lesson, Rhett," the first young man said.

"Yeah, teach him a lesson," the other two men both said at the same time.

Nicolas inhaled a deep breath, closing his eyes. Sure, this part of the job was always the fun part. He loved it when he could prove a man who thought he was bigger or better than him wrong. It was a perk that came with not only the badge but just being him. Still, with every lesson, there was a chance or risk of it going badly. He wanted to make his point to a man challenging him, but that didn't mean he wanted to hurt or kill the man.

Rhett approached the table, and as he reached Nicolas's side, Nicolas rose to his feet. His chair fell to the ground as he grabbed Rhett's throat with his hand, squeezing it. Rhett froze and gasped for breath. He tried to wave his arms and hit Nicolas, but Nicolas picked the man up, slamming him to the ground. Rhett gasped for breath even more. His eyes widened as he seemed to realize he'd made a mistake approaching the table in the manner in which he did.

His three friends jumped to their feet, and Nicolas yanked his gun from his holster, pointing it in Rhett's face. "One step from any of you, and I will blow his head off. Understand?"

They each moved another step, but Rhett shouted for them to stop.

"Now, you see this badge?" Nicolas asked him, showing Rhett his Pinkerton badge. "This says that you are to leave these three women alone. Do you understand?"

"Yes."

"Yes, what?"

"Yes, Sir."

"Good. I want you and your men to leave. Right now."

"Yes, Sir." Rhett nodded, and as Nicolas released him, he scrambled out from under the Pinkerton that was twice his size. Rhett darted toward his friends, and the four ran from the fort without looking over their shoulders.

Nicolas watched them until they vanished before turning to the women.

"Thank you, Sir," the mother said.

"My pleasure, ma'am." He tipped his hat and went back to his table, sitting down before taking another bite of chili.

THREE

NICOLAS

*N*icolas's horse galloped through the tall grass. He'd patrolled the land around Fort Boise for the last several days, searching through the trees and mountains for any sign of a makeshift camp or anyone he could come across. None of the few strangers he caught up with not only were the man he was looking for, though, nor had any of them seen him.

He didn't want to think about how he was trying to find a needle in a haystack, but the truth of it was, that was exactly what he was doing.

Course, this wasn't his first needle.

He had found men before—men who were thought to be impossible to find.

And he would do it again.

A gunshot echoed throughout the mountains, and he yanked his horse to a stop. The horse grunted, throwing its head at the sudden movement. Another shot cracked, then a third, a fourth, and a fifth. Nicolas furrowed his brow and spurred the horse into a gallop toward the mountains.

*W*ith several more shots, it didn't take long before he scaled over the hill and came upon a woman standing in a clearing. Her back was to him, and her long fire-red curls moved in the slight breeze. She stood several yards from a dead tree that had fallen, and as he halted his horse to watch her, she pointed a gun at the tree and shot it, hitting the stump of a branch sticking up from the trunk.

Nice shot, he thought.

Her horse lifted his head, turning toward him and his horse, and as it nickered, she spun, facing Nicolas.

Her eyes widened then her brow furrowed. She dropped her hands to her waist but kept ahold of the pistol.

Nicolas held up his hands. "I just heard the gunshots and thought I would check out what was going on," he said.

She nodded, and although the tension in her shoulders softened, she studied him as he cued his horse in a slow walk toward her.

"I'm Nicolas Kelly." He moved his jacket, exposing his badge. "I'm a Pinkerton in the area and heard the shots."

She nodded again. "Charlotte McLaren. I'm just passing through on a wagon train camped nearby, and I was doing a little bit of target practice." Her Irish accent purred, and she blinked her bright green eyes at him. His heart thumped, and he sucked in a breath.

What on earth is wrong with me, he thought.

He tipped his hat. "It's a pleasure to meet you, Miss McLaren. Or is it Mrs.?"

"No. It's Miss."

A hint of relief washed through him, and his mind scoffed at it.

Why on earth would I care if she was a Miss or Mrs.?

He swung his leg over the saddle to dismount but paused. "Do you mind?" he asked her.

She shook her head, and he stepped down to the ground and moved around to the front of his horse, shifting the reins from one hand to the other behind his back. "So, target practice. Are you practicing your skills for hunting?"

Her lips twitched into a half smile, and she glanced down to her feet before looking back at him. "Something like that."

He looked out at the log she'd shot. "Well, you're a good shot. Kind of close range for hunting, though, and of course, the tree isn't moving."

She raised one eyebrow, giving him a sideways glance.

He cleared his throat. "But it's still a really good shot." Heat rushed up the back of his neck. He hadn't meant to offend the woman, but his mouth talked before he had a chance to hear himself.

What an idiot, he thought. *You just met the woman, and you're already offending her.*

"Well," she said. "I have been shooting since I was six years old. I think I can handle meself. Don't know if yeh could say the same. But I guess I'll take yer word for it." She wiggled her nose, and through the half smile on her lips, there was a patronizing hint to her tone.

"I suppose I deserve that," he said, chuckling.

"You suppose correctly," she said, raising one eyebrow again. "So, yer decent then?"

"Yeah, you could say that. Being a Pinkerton, we are trained to be. A weapon is a difference between life and death for us sometimes."

"That still doesn't mean yeh have better aim." She pointed toward the fallen tree. "So, if yeh want to prove it, then?"

A smile spread across his lips as he shrugged his shoulders. Surely, he wanted to do just that, but at what cost? He never wanted to show rudeness just to be right. Yet, there was an odd sense to her dare as though she wanted him to take it because it was just as fun for her as it was for him.

"All right. Care to make a wager on it?" he asked.

"And what will yeh give me when I win?"

He snorted a laugh. "Your confidence does nothing to intimidate me or impress me."

"I didn't think it did, but yeh didn't answer me question. What will yeh give me when I win?"

He folded his arms across his chest and cocked his head to the side. "I don't know. You are a stranger, after all. What will you give me when I win?"

She tapped her lips with her index finger for a moment before a broad grin spread across her face, and she made her way to her horse, fetching something from her saddle bag.

"I have this." She opened her hand, and a gold nugget lay in her palm.

Of course, it was a prize and one worth winning. But looking at it caused a wash of guilt through his chest. He couldn't take something so valuable from her. It wouldn't be right. It wouldn't be gentlemanly.

"How about we shoot for bragging rights?"

She cocked her head to the side. "Bragging rights? That doesn't seem valuable."

"Well, I think it does. I mean, if you win—*and that's a big if*—you could tell people you bested a Pinkerton. What could be more valuable than that?"

She inhaled a deep breath, shrugging. "All right. Bragging rights, it is."

∼

CHARLOTTE

"So, what are we shooting at?" Charlotte hooked the trigger guard of her pistol on her finger and spun it around several times.

The Pinkerton smiled, and her heartbeat kicked up. She wanted to ignore the ruggedness throughout every inch of him and how his long chocolate-colored hair framed his chiseled jawline. Every bit the pictured image she imagined a Pinkerton to be, his broad shoulders and height towered over her.

"Um . . . well, why not the targets you were using? There's that branch and that one." He pointed out several more. "How do all of those sound?"

A hint of nervousness twisted in her stomach, and she nodded, straightening her shoulders in hopes of hiding even the slightest notion of unease to her. She was confident, yet she'd never been under pressure from someone other than herself to do well.

"Are you ready?" the Pinkerton asked.

"Always."

He chuckled. "Well, then by all means . . ."

With a deep inhaled breath, she pointed her pistol at the first target and fired. One by one, she hit every single one, blowing the bark off the different tree branches.

"Not bad," the Pinkerton said after she finished. "Now, can you hit them all with your left hand?"

"I guess yeh will find out." Although boastful in her voice, a tiny rush of dread brushed against her nerves. Although she was accomplished with her right hand, her left hand had always proved a different story.

She reloaded the pistol and readied to shoot once more. No matter how many calming breaths she took, however, one by one, she missed several of the targets. Each round of gunfire thumped in her chest and deafened her ears, the sound drowning out the slew of groans vibrating through her chest.

"Left-handed is always harder." The Pinkerton ducked his chin and lowered his voice as though to hide even the slightest hint of arrogance about him.

"Quite," she growled.

Her stomach twisted into knots as the Pinkerton loaded his gun, and the flawless lines of his stance set fire to the only chance she had of coming out of this the victorious one—a hope that soon vanished while she watched him hit every mark with his right hand and then his left hand, perfectly. His aim far surpassed hers.

Through her irritation, she couldn't help but laugh as the Pinkerton approached her, and with his hands resting on both of the holstered pistols, he slowed his steps and rocked his hips. Pride shined in every curve of his grin, yet it held a cautious modesty as though unsure exactly how mad she'd be.

"Just decent, huh?" she asked, cocking her head to the side.

He shrugged. "Perhaps I understated myself a bit."

"A bit?"

"In all fairness, you took on a Pinkerton."

"Aye. I suppose yer right. Bloody fool I am." She chuckled.

"I have to admit, though, I was a bit nervous. I thought maybe I'd challenged someone I shouldn't have."

"Liar," she laughed.

He tipped his hat, and her cheeks flushed with warmth. "I can assure you, ma'am, that I wouldn't lie about that."

"Charlotte! Charlotte! Where are yeh?" a voice called out.

Uncle Ned popped out from some bushes. His hat sat on the side of his head, and his hair was all disheveled as though he'd been fighting the plant and lost. "Bloody bushes." He slapped at the branches, stumbling backward from them as he brushed at his jacket and pants. "Charlotte!"

"Over here, Uncle Ned," she called back to him.

He spun and looked at her, his mouth gaping open as he seemed to take in the man standing next to her. "I . . . I didn't know yeh had company."

"Uncle Ned, this is . . . Mr. Kelly. He's a Pinkerton in the area, and he happened upon me after hearing my gunshots. I suppose he thought I was in trouble or something."

Uncle Ned snorted. "Yeh? *In* trouble?" He looked at Mr. Kelly. "More like she's the cause of the trouble."

Mr. Kelly laughed.

Charlotte didn't. "Har. Har. Uncle. Yer hilarious."

"Aye, I am." Uncle Ned winked, then moved toward Mr. Kelly with his hand outstretched. "It's a pleasure to meet yeh."

"You too." Mr. Kelly backed away from the two of them. "I should let you two get back to your wagon train." He returned to his horse, climbing back in the saddle. "Thank you for the . . . interesting afternoon, Miss McLaren."

"Yer welcome. Thank you for showing me I need to work on shooting with me left hand."

He spun his horse and cued it into a trot. She watched the horse and the Pinkerton until they vanished from her sight. Part of her didn't know what to make of what had happened, and the other part wished it would happen all over again.

"Care to tell me what happened?" Uncle Ned asked.

"Nothing happened. He happened upon me, we spoke, we shot a few rounds, and he left."

Uncle Ned's eyes narrowed, and he pointed toward her. "Don't be thinking yeh can lie to me, Lass. I know yeh better than that."

"I'm not lying."

Uncle Ned continued studying her. "I don't believe yeh."

"Well, it doesn't matter if yeh do or not, does it now?" She turned away from her uncle, glancing up at the sky as she said a prayer he wouldn't see right through her, knowing she was not only lying but trying to hide it.

Of course, it was foolish to think about Mr. Kelly. Surely, she would never see him again. Besides, she had other priorities. The only man she should be thinking about was Jack Carter.

Period.

FOUR

NICOLAS

$\mathcal{N}$icolas found himself smiling every time he thought of the crazy redhead in the forest as he rode back to the fort, ate dinner, spent the night under the stars, and then while he ate breakfast the next day. He didn't want to think about her, but he couldn't help it. He just did. He thought about how she smiled, how her hair fell in her eyes when she concentrated, and how her Irish accent rolled off her tongue. She'd captivated him, and he didn't even know how.

He didn't even know that someone could.

Surely, he thought about love and marriage, about finding a woman to marry and start a family. But he was a Pinkerton. Pinkertons tended to stay away from all of that. Or at least he had. His job was dangerous and took him far away to distant towns and cities, not returning home for months and months at a time.

What kind of a life would that be for a wife and children, he thought. Not seeing her husband or their father for months at a time. *No, I couldn't do that to someone. I refuse to chain someone to a life like that.*

He grimaced as he looked down at the eggs and strips of

bacon. He'd been hungry when he sat down to eat them, but now he wasn't sure he even wanted them. He leaned back in his chair, tossing the fork on the plate before folding his arms across his chest.

The fort was busy already that morning with immigrants meandering all around to the different supply tents, buying and gathering what they would need for the last stretch before Oregon. While others were handing over cash, even more were loading up their wagons with different sacks of dried goods, extra wagon wheels, and some even threw in rifles and ammunition.

"You can never be too careful," he heard one man say. "Lots of drifters out there ready to steal what they can from any wagon trains passing through."

Nicolas furrowed his brow and then dug into his pocket, yanking out the wanted picture of Jack Carter. Not only had other Pinkertons been on the hunt for this man, but Nicolas had spent nearly four months traveling across several states, searching throughout any town or fort he came across and asking everyone he came into contact with.

But he hadn't checked the wagon trains.

Furthermore, he hadn't asked them.

A groan vibrated through his lips.

Of course, he thought. *Even with dozens of men—and even more guns—a criminal could sneak in at night and take what he needed, whether it be a sack of flour or even a cow. Or one could approach them in broad daylight, giving them a sob story about losing his family to cholera and how he's on his own.*

Nicolas slapped his forehead.

How could he have been so stupid?

He shoved the plate away from him, watching it slide across the table as he rose to his feet. A few men who were eating at different tables around him all stopped and stared, and he ignored them as he slid his arms into his jacket and placed his hat on his head.

"Well, I'm not going to be stupid anymore," he whispered to himself. "I've got to find a wagon train to join."

~

*A*lthough he had asked a few wagon masters around the fort, none of them seemed too keen on letting him join, and while some considered it for longer than others, one by one, they all shook their heads.

"I don't want to bring unwanted attention to the group," one said.

"I don't think it's a good idea," another said.

"I don't want to get involved in messes like that," a third said.

It wasn't until he approached the fourth, a scruffy-looking man who had just arrived at the fort with his weary-looking travelers, that Nicolas got an answer other than no.

"I can't say I know much about coming across any wanted men. We haven't had much trouble on the trail with the exception of some bandits back in Nebraska . . . or perhaps it was Kansas. I'm not sure. To be honest, most days all seem to be the same. That's what happens out here, though." The wagon master scratched his chin as he looked over the wanted picture Nicolas had handed him. "But you're more than welcome to ask around."

"And what if I wanted to join you?"

The wagon master furrowed his brow. "Well, I don't think there would be a problem with that. But I got no extra supplies to feed you."

"You wouldn't have to worry about that."

"Then I got no problem with it." The wagon master outstretched his hand. "The name's Mr. Russell, and welcome to the wagon train."

"Thank you." Nicolas shook the man's hand and then headed back into the fort to pack his things. Why he didn't think to join a wagon train until now, he'll never know, but he couldn't help but feel one step closer to finding Jack Carter.

∼

CHARLOTTE

Of all the faces Charlotte had ever seen, she'd never forgotten the one she looked for everywhere. Strangers came and went; people who pass by her in a blink of an eye meant nothing to her.

But there was one who did.

And she looked for him everywhere.

Jack Carter's face was so burned in Charlotte's memory that there were times she could remember him more than her own Pa. She didn't like that, but that was the truth of the matter. While Uncle Ned always told her to forget about him and what happened, she never could. Of course, she understood why her uncle said what he did. He wanted her to find peace in her life, and even if she couldn't forgive and forget fully, he wanted her to forgive enough.

"If that makes sense," he would say.

Although it did, there were times she didn't want it to.

She didn't want to think that she lived her life in a sea of regret and pain, but if she were to be honest, that was exactly where she dwelled, along with hints of anger. She didn't want to live there for the rest of her life, but she knew that the only freedom she would have would come through finding and killing Jack Carter.

Period.

Once he was no longer walking the earth . . . that was when she would find peace.

Charlotte meandered through the maze of people in the fort, heading toward one of the supply tents. They only needed a few things for the last stretch to Oregon, and with Mr. Russell planning on just camping for the night and leaving at dawn, she wanted to get the things they needed that morning so they could get them packed before the wagon train headed out.

She entered the tent, glancing around at the different shelves of stacked supplies, and with a list in her hand, she headed toward a man who was in the corner of the tent, talking to another man.

"I'll be by to pick the supplies up in an hour," the man with his back to her said.

"Of course, Mr. Kelly. I will have it all ready for you." The owner of the supply tent wiped his brow, and there was a tremble in his voice as though he was intimidated by the man standing in front of him.

The man turned and sucked in a breath as he glanced down at Charlotte. "You."

She looked up, meeting the same green eyes as she had in the mountains. "The Pinkerton," she said before she could think about his name. Warmth spread through her cheeks, and she cleared her throat. "I mean, Mr. Kelly."

"You remembered." He wiggled his finger at her, closing one eye. "Miss McLaren."

"Yeh remembered."

"How could I forget?"

Another wave of heat warmed through her cheeks, this time running down the back of her neck. Her heart thumped.

"I trust your morning is going well," he said.

"It is. And yers?" She wasn't sure what kind of small talk they were making, but it seemed rude not to ask.

"It is. Or at least it will be after I gather all the supplies I need."

"Me too." She held out the small piece of paper in her hand. "After I get what I need."

"Well, then, I'll let you get to it." He tipped his hat and turned to leave, pausing for a second as he waved to someone behind her. She glanced over her shoulder, catching sight of Mr. Russell. Her brow furrowed.

"Do you know Mr. Russell?" she asked.

"The wagon master? Yes." He nodded.

Her heart kicked up a beat again.

As if to hear the conversation, Mr. Russell approached them, removing his hat as he reached their side. The trail hadn't been easy on him just as with every other man traveling. In the months they had traveled he'd grown a full beard, and his clothes were stained with sweat and the dirt of each state they had traveled through. "Good afternoon, Miss McLaren, Mr. Kelly," the wagon master said.

"Good afternoon, Mr. Russell." Mr. Kelly motioned toward the supply tent owner. "Just ordered my supplies, so I'll be ready to head out at dawn."

Did I just hear the Pinkerton correctly?

"Yer traveling with our wagon train?" Charlotte asked, furrowing her brow.

"*Our?*" Mr. Kelly glanced between her and the wagon master. Hesitation hinted in the way he looked upon each of them as though he thought she implied that she and Mr. Russell were together.

"No, not ours," she said, waving her hand. "I mean, his." A slight chuckle whispered through her breath. "It's his wagon train. I'm just traveling with my uncle."

Mr. Russell tucked his chin, smiling for a moment before he cleared his throat. "Well, I'll let you two get back to your afternoons. I will see you both at dawn."

The wagon master turned and headed out of the tent.

Although she couldn't be sure, Charlotte thought she heard him laugh the whole way.

"Well, I should let you get to your supplies." Mr. Kelly tipped his hat again and Charlotte bit her lip.

"Are yeh really gonna be traveling on my wagon train?" she asked.

"Just for a bit ma'am."

"Can yeh tell me why?"

"I'm looking for a man that's been rumored to be in the area. If he's traveling without much, then I believe he will target wagon trains for food and other supplies he needs."

Not another run in with bandits, she thought. *Once was enough.*

"I see," she said. "Well, I suppose I'll see yeh at dawn."

He smiled and turned toward the flap of the tent. She watched him until he vanished, and she sucked in a breath.

"Ma'am? Ma'am?" a voice caught her attention, and she turned toward the tent owner. "How can I help ya?" he asked.

"Oh, I . . . I . . . I can't remember what I came in here for." She shook her head, closing her eyes. Mr. Kelly had distracted her just enough that she'd forgotten what she needed.

"Is it written down on that scrap of paper?" the owner asked.

She glanced down, looking at her uncle's chicken scratch handwriting. "Oh. Yes. It is." She handed it to the tent owner. "I need these supplies."

"And will ya be taking them now or picking them up?"

"Um. Now." She glanced at the flap again where Mr. Kelly had disappeared. "I'll take them now."

FIVE

CHARLOTTE

The wagon rolled down the trail as Charlotte sat on the buckboard with her uncle. Their shoulders brushed together as the wheels rolled over rocks and twigs, shifting the wagon along with the terrain. Her rump ached, and with each bump, she closed her eyes.

"I heard we got a new traveler with us," her uncle said, casting her a sideways glance.

"Aye. I heard that too." She ignored the hint of amusement in her uncle's voice.

"And did yeh hear who it was?"

"Um." She glanced up at the sky, not wanting to answer the question but knowing she had to. She knew there wasn't a chance he was gonna let her ignore him or his question. "I think it's a Pinkerton or some man."

"Not just a Pinkerton. It's the one you met the other day while shooting."

"Oh. Aye. That's what I heard."

"Have yeh spoken to him?" Uncle Ned glanced at her again. He played off his question as nothing more than an innocent one, yet it was the furthest thing from innocent as it could get.

For a moment, she thought about lying. How would he know if she had or hadn't spoken to him? He wasn't in the supply tent in the fort. Nor did she mention it when she returned to the wagon. She hadn't wanted to for this very reason and the conversation she was having right now. Not to mention, but when they had spoken, nothing was said, really. Just mindless chit-chat interrupted by Mr. Russell. She would hardly even call what little was said between them a conversation. Even with all of that, she still hated the thought of lying.

"I saw him at the fort, and he mentioned traveling with the wagon train, but only for a little way. I guess he's looking for someone, but I didn't ask for any details about it."

"What else did yeh two speak about?"

"That was it, really. I don't even consider it a conversation. It was a passing hello, then that he was traveling with the wagon train looking for someone, and then goodbye. Nothing more."

"Yer just like yer father. Yeh know that, right?"

"And just what is that supposed to mean?"

Uncle Ned snorted a tiny laugh and shook his head. "I remember the day yer father met yer mother. We were walking through town, headed to the pub, when she walked by, pushing her bicycle. Of course, I suggested we stop and see if the lass needed help. I could tell he wanted to stop, but he waved off me suggestion. He tipped his hat, of course, but he didn't stop. Not until she turned to us and asked if we could help."

Uncle Ned chuckled as though he was picturing the whole scene in his mind. Charlotte couldn't help but try to do the same. Even if she knew nothing about the town they lived in or even anything about Ireland. They immigrated to the United States a few years after she was born, and she had little memory of the country.

"After we helped her, I invited her to the pub, and she came with us. I could tell there was a spark between them, and I think yer mother could, too. But yer father . . . he was a stubborn mule. He kept insisting he didn't think of her in such a way. We all knew he was."

Charlotte's stomach clenched and twisted. She really hated how insightful her uncle was most of the time. "Well, that's a wonderful story, but that's not like me."

Uncle Ned snorted another laugh, cocking his head to the side. "If yeh say so, Lass."

His accusations clawed at her insides, yet she couldn't bring herself to say anything more. She didn't want to continue defending her stance, for it only made her look more guilty, and nothing could be worse for her.

The wagon in front of them stopped, and Uncle Ned pulled their horses to a halt. "I wonder what's going on," he said.

"I wonder if someone has a broken wheel."

Uncle Ned let out a groan. "I sure hope not. I'm not in the mood to change a bloody wheel this afternoon."

The two jumped down from the wagon, and along with everyone else behind them, they made their way toward the front of the wagon train. As they neared the front, they heard shouts from several travelers, and Charlotte's pace quickened.

"Charlotte! Over here!" Emma waved her hand while Abby rushed to the other side of Lillian's wagon.

"What's wrong?" Charlotte asked.

"It's Lillian." Emma grabbed Charlotte's hand and led her around to the other side of the wagon too.

Lillian sat on the ground next to the wheel. With Everett on one side of her and her mother on the other, she held onto her belly and screamed. She looked up at Charlotte with just her eyes, and tears filled them.

"I'm scared," she whispered.

Charlotte knelt beside her. "Don't be. Everything will be all right."

"I wish Sadie was here."

A small part of Charlotte's heart broke. She didn't know how many times she'd uttered those same words, but if she guessed, it would be in the thousands. "I do too."

"You were with Sadie when she helped Mrs. Baker, weren't you?" Lillian's mother asked.

"Yes, I was."

"So, can you help my daughter?"

Charlotte sucked in a breath. "I'm not a midwife."

"Neither am I."

"But yeh've had a child."

"Decades ago."

"Could you two stop arguing and just help my wife!" Everett's voice boomed over the two of them, and as Charlotte looked at the fear in his eyes, her heart sank.

"Of course," she said. "I need a bucket of hot water and a couple of blankets."

He nodded and jumped to his feet, rushing around to the other side of the wagon. The rest of the travelers dispersed, giving Lillian and the women helping her room without watchful eyes that had no business being around, and while the wagons moved away from them, circling to make a campsite several yards away, the four women helped Lillian move over so she could prop herself up against one of the wheels.

After Everett returned with the items they needed, he made his way around to the other side of the wagon, running his hands through his hair several times while he blew out a couple of breaths. Emma ran after him, and although Charlotte couldn't hear what the sister was saying to her brother, it wasn't hard to figure out.

Charlotte knelt beside Lillian. "Lift."

Lillian did as she was told, lifting her rump off the ground while Charlotte slid the blanket under her. The laboring woman groaned and closed her eyes.

"What if I don't make it?" she whispered.

"Yeh will do fine. Don't think about such nonsense. In a few hours, yer gonna be holding that baby with a smile on yer face, and all this will be a distant memory."

Lillian moaned again. She covered her face with her hands for a moment before she rolled over onto her side and then drew her body up, propping herself on her hands and knees. She rocked back and forth, blowing out deep breaths. Her body, drenched in sweat, trembled. Her stomach clenched in a ball, and she closed her eyes, hissing a deep breath through her gritted teeth. She screamed. The pain seemed to spread through her whole body until, finally, her tight shoulders softened. She panted with heavy breaths, wiping the sweat from her brow. Her dampened curls stuck to the back of her neck.

Contraction after contraction, the four women helped Lillian move in a constant dance from one position to another, whether on her back, on her hands and knees, or squatting.

Minutes turned into more. Five, ten, perhaps even as many as what would make up an hour and then another one, had passed while Charlotte paid close attention to Lillian's painful moans. She didn't want to admit that while she was with Sadie when she helped Mrs. Baker, Charlotte had ignored most of what was going on. It wasn't that she didn't care to know, but it scared her to know. Abby and Emma, along with Lillian's mother, just sat and watched. Their eyes were wide with wonder and concern.

"I can feel something. I think . . . I think it is coming!" Lillian shouted. The explosion of her tone caused Charlotte to flinch, and Lillian belted out another scream. Her whole body tightened. "It is coming." She shifted back on her hands and knees, her weight leaned back onto her hips, and with one last loud groan, a baby slid onto the blanket.

Lillian's mother scooped up the baby, wrapping it tightly as the new mother collapsed forward, rolling over onto her back.

Her skin paled, and her eyes rolled backward until Charlotte could only see the whites. Her pupils vanished. She gasped for a few breaths then her body went limp.

"Lillian? Lillian!" her mother shouted.

Charlotte grabbed the bucket of water, dunking a cloth in it before wiping Lillian's face.

"What's wrong with her?" Lillian's mother asked.

"She's just tired." Charlotte glanced at Emma and Abby. "Can you take the baby and wash her?"

"Her?" Emma gushed, brushing her fingers against her chest. "I hadn't noticed. I have a niece?"

"Yes, yeh do, now take the baby and bloody wash her." A slight growl vibrated through Charlotte's chest as she continued wiping the wet cloth over Lillian's face. They would have plenty of time to gush over the baby once her mother gained consciousness.

While Abby moved over to Lillian and grabbed her hand, holding it, Emma took the infant from Lillian's mother, who crawled over to Lillian and Charlotte.

"Is she going to . . . die?" Lillian's mother asked.

"I don't think so. I think she is just weak from the pain."

While Charlotte continued tending to Lillian, Emma laid the infant on the blanket and took another cloth, dunking it in the water so she could clean the baby.

"What do I do about this?" She pointed toward the umbilical cord.

"Cut it," Charlotte said.

Abby jumped to her feet, rushing to the wagon to find a knife. After securing one, she rushed over to Emma and the baby. Emma took the knife and cut the cord, tying the end. Her face scrunched with mild disgust, and with that task done, she began pouring the warmed water over the infant as Abby scrubbed her wrinkled body and the tiny head full of jet-black hair. The baby's legs kicked, and with her eyes clamped shut, she cried as though she was in pain, even though she wasn't.

Lillian finally stirred awake as if jarred back to consciousness from her daughter's cries. She blinked for a few seconds before sitting up and leaning back against the wheel again. She coughed with several dry heaves.

"Stay there and don't move," Charlotte ordered.

"But the baby."

"She is all right. Emma will bring her to yeh."

"She? I have a daughter?"

As Lillian kept whispering for her daughter, Emma wrapped the girl in a blanket and placed her on her mother's chest. The baby's shrill cries soon turned into soft coos and grunts while in her mother's arms, and with a deep exhaled breath, Lillian laid her head down. Her eyes fluttered for a second before she fell to sleep. Her breaths deepened as the baby napped upon her chest.

"May I get Everett now?" Emma asked. She had a slight bounce to her step as she grinned from ear to ear.

"Yeah. I think that would be good."

~

With the new family tucked away in the wagon for the night, the rest of the camp kept to themselves, eating supper and spending time around their own campfires before turning in. Although Charlotte was exhausted, there was an edge to her emotions that left her wide awake, and she sat in front of the fire, watching the flames even long after everyone else went to sleep.

"Care for some company?" a voice asked.

She glanced up from the fire as Mr. Kelly walked toward her.

"What are yeh doing awake? Shouldn't yeh be asleep?"

"Funny. I could ask you the same thing."

"True." She glanced at the fire and then back at him before motioning for him to sit on the log next to her. "I suppose I shouldn't have said that."

"Eh. Seems like a natural thing to wonder, given I didn't go through the . . . excitement of the afternoon like you did."

"I suppose that's true too."

He sat down, exhaling a deep breath. "I was impressed with what you did today."

"Thank you."

"I didn't know you knew what to do."

Charlotte snorted. "I didn't. I watched a friend of mine who is a doctor help a woman give birth, but honestly, I didn't really know what I was doing."

"Well, it didn't seem like that, and now that family is sleeping happily and healthy. You did good."

"Do yeh have a wife and children, Mr. Kelly?" She glanced over at him, unsure why she asked him what she did.

He shook his head. "Nah."

"So, yeh never wanted to marry?"

"No, it's not that I never wanted to or don't want to now. I just . . . a lot is going on in my life."

"I can understand that."

"Is that why you aren't married?"

His question made her heart thump. "Aye. It is."

They both fell silent as they watched the fire. Although it should have been an awkward silence, it wasn't. Instead, Charlotte almost felt calm. As though they both found a peaceful quiet sitting next to one another. She almost didn't want them to speak at all, finding pleasure in the stillness of the night.

"I don't wish to interrupt the quiet, but I have to say, I kind of like just sitting here, saying nothing . . . with you." Mr. Kelly glanced at her and smiled.

"Aye, I know. I like it too."

"I guess I won't say anything else then. I wouldn't want to spoil it."

"It's all right." She fought a yawn and lost. Her eyes fluttered, and her head got heavy. She leaned and swayed, and as she closed her eyes, her head found something to lay on as she drifted to sleep.

SIX

CHARLOTTE

Someone cleared their throat, and Charlotte's eyes fluttered a few times, then opened. She sat up, glancing to her right and then in front of her.

"Good morning." Uncle Ned said. He stood in front of her with his arms folded across his chest. Emma and Abby stood with him. Their eyes were wide as they blinked. Abby even had her hand over her mouth.

Charlotte rubbed her eyes, glancing to her right again, and she jerked back as she noticed Mr. Kelly sitting next to her. His head drooped, tucked against his chin as he slept.

She looked back at her uncle, Emma, and Abby. "Good morning," she said. "Are . . . are we leaving camp?"

"Not this morning. Mr. Russell agreed to wait a couple of days to help Mr. and Mrs. Ford with the birth of their daughter."

Charlotte looked at Emma and Abby. "Is . . . is Lillian all right?"

"She's sore, but otherwise all right," Emma said as she glanced between Charlotte and Mr. Kelly.

Charlotte elbowed the Pinkerton, and he snorted and

jerked awake. He blinked several times as he looked at everyone standing around them then he looked at Charlotte.

"What happened?" he asked.

"We fell asleep," Charlotte said with a slight growl to her voice. It wasn't because she was irritated they had fallen asleep, it was more because she was irritated they'd gotten caught, and by the look on Uncle Ned's face, he wasn't about to let her live this one down.

"Oh." Mr. Kelly cleared his throat and rubbed his face with his hands before standing. He stretched his back and arms. "Well, I suppose I should get to . . ." He pointed toward the other side of the camp. "Whatever I have to do. I should tack up my horse and patrol."

Before anyone could say a word to him, he strode off, heading across the camp. Charlotte watched him for a moment before she dropped her gaze to the ground.

"I should probably check on Lillian this morning," she said, clearing her throat.

Just as Mr. Kelly had walked off before anyone could say anything, Charlotte made her way to Lillian's wagon, keeping her head down and not stopping until she reached her destination. Although she sensed Emma and Abby following close behind her, she didn't look over her shoulder, nor did she say anything to them when the three finally arrived at Lillian's wagon.

"Good morning," she said to Everett as she approached.

The new father was kneeling by the fire, tending to the charred chunks of wood while it heated a pot of coffee. He looked worn, and he rubbed his face, blinking at her as though he hadn't slept all night.

"Good morning," he said.

"Dear brother, did you not sleep at all?" Emma asked. He shook his head, and she moved over to him, laying her hand on his shoulder. "Why don't you go to my wagon and get some rest? We will stay with Lillian and the baby."

He nodded, giving her a mumbled response that Charlotte couldn't hear before he staggered off, weaving his way toward Emma's wagon.

Charlotte watched him as she had Mr. Kelly for a moment before heading toward the back of the Ford's wagon and peeking her head around the corner.

"Good morning," she said to Lillian.

Lillian lifted her head from the pillow and smiled. "Good morning."

"May I come in?"

"Of course."

Charlotte climbed into the wagon, settling down next to her friend. "How are yeh feeling this morning?"

"Tired."

"I can imagine."

"I want to get out of this wagon and stretch my legs."

"I think that would be good."

"Everett won't let me move."

Charlotte waved her hand. "Well, he's gone, so . . ." She jerked her head toward the opening of the wagon and smiled.

Lillian smiled too, and as Charlotte took the baby from her, Lillian lifted the blanket from her body and slowly made her way out of the wagon. She hissed a few times as though it would lessen the pain, and after stepping down onto the ground, she spun, reaching out to take the baby back.

"Give me a minute with her," Charlotte said, winking.

"All right."

The two walked over to the campfire where Emma and Abby sat, tending to the fire and finishing the coffee Everett started. Lillian took her place beside Emma, wincing as she sat on the log, while Charlotte sat next to Abby. The baby squirmed a little in her arms and scrunched her face as though she thought about crying but settled without making a sound and fell back to sleep.

"So, what did yeh name her?" Charlotte asked Lillian.

"Marie Sofia Ford."

"That's lovely." Charlotte looked down upon the wee little lass. "Hello, Marie, and how are yeh doing this fine morning?"

"Challenging her mamma," Lillian answered.

The four women chuckled.

"She's not even a day old; how much work can she be?" Abby asked.

"I'll let you answer that the day after you have your baby." Lillian motioned toward Abby's growing bump.

Charlotte looked down at the baby again, moving the blanket away from her face. She couldn't help but feel a twinge of longing.

"If you keep looking at that baby like that, you're going to make me think there's something more serious going on between you and that Pinkerton," Emma said.

Charlotte's heart thumped. "I don't know what yer talking about. I'm just admiring the little lass's beauty."

"What is she talking about?" Lillian asked, glancing between Emma and Charlotte.

"Charlotte was sleeping with her head on the Pinkerton's shoulder this morning. Apparently, they were talking last night and fell asleep. I mean, that's what it seemed like. Care to enlighten us on what happened, Charlotte?"

Her heart thumped even harder. "Nothing happened."

"So, you were asleep, and he just happened to sit down next to you and fall asleep too?"

"No. 'Twasn't like that." Charlotte's Irish accent got a little thicker. "I was sitting by the fire, and he couldn't sleep either, so he sat down. We talked a bit, and then I must have fallen asleep. 'Twas purely nothing more than a conversation between acquaintances."

"Acquaintances?" Emma raised one eyebrow and cocked her head to the side.

"Aye. It's not like we're friends. I barely know him."

"But do you want to get to know him?"

"Yeh know I don't have time for all that." Charlotte waved her hand at Emma.

"But you could have. If you . . . decided, it was what you wanted instead . . . instead of . . ."

"Instead of trying to find the man I'm looking for?" Charlotte tucked her chin, lowering her voice. "That's not an option."

"But what if—"

"No. No, but what if's. Sadie always tried to talk me out of searching for the man. She always tried to tell me I needed to live my life as happily as I could. Even Uncle Ned has said that; I don't know how many times. But I'm not gonna listen . . . to any of yeh."

"We don't mean to upset you, Charlotte," Abby said.

"Yeh didn't." Charlotte shook her head. "And I don't mean to yell either. I just . . . I can't think of anything else because if I do . . . then I don't know what the last nearly fifteen years of my life has been lived for."

There it was, the honest answer she had often told herself but had never told another person.

Since she was five, the only thing she'd thought of or worked toward was finding Jack Carter. She hadn't thought of anything else, hadn't considered anything else. Although it didn't lose much priority, her schooling was all done through the eyes of a girl only caring about one thing, which was never learning how to read, write, or do arithmetic, and during her young adult life, while her friends were going to society parties and holiday dances with dancing cards on their wrists and hopes of young gentlemen in their hearts, she passed on them, never allowing herself one evening of the fun they all seemed to have.

She was far too busy for dancing.

She was far too busy for young gentlemen.

She was far too busy for love.

And she was all right with those things.

She didn't care.

But if she were to care now and to suddenly give up on everything she's ever lived for . . .

What would be the purpose of her life?

What would be the purpose of everything?

"You are more than the death of your father, Charlotte. If that was who you were or what your life was all about, then I would be nothing but the jilted daughter of a swindler, and my life would be nothing but the bad choices he made with his money." Emma glanced at Lillian. "And so would Everett."

"Do you want to get to know Mr. Kelly?" Abby asked. "He is quite handsome."

Charlotte's brows furrowed as she glanced at her. "It's not that simple."

"But it is, Charlotte," Lillian said. "Trust me."

"I agree." Emma nodded, looking between the two women. "It is."

Charlotte furrowed her brow again at the honest answers sitting on the tip of her tongue. Mr. Kelly was intriguing.

"Suppose he does interest me," she said. "What should I do if he doesn't share the same feelings?"

"He came over to your camp when he knew you were awake, and he not only let you fall asleep on his shoulder, but after you did, instead of waking you, he spent the night sleeping, sitting up next to you." Emma chuckled. "I don't doubt that he feels the same. Or at least does a little."

"Perhaps you should talk to him," Abby said. "Or if you want one of us to talk to him."

"No. No. That's not what I want." For the first time in she didn't know how long, Charlotte began to think about life after finding Mr. Carter. The problem was that since she never thought about it, she couldn't picture it now.

"I should see if my uncle needs help this morning." She stood, and after kissing the baby on the cheek, she handed her over to her mother. "Let me know if yeh need anything."

"Are you sure you don't want to stay for a little longer?" Lillian asked, looking up at Charlotte as she took her daughter back into her arms.

"I'm sure."

"We didn't mean to upset you," Emma said.

"I'm not upset." Charlotte leaned over and laid her hand on Emma's shoulder. "It's nothing any of yeh did. It's my own demons."

"We would love to help you with those."

"Aye. I know. But they are mine. I must fight them on me own."

SEVEN

NICOLAS

$\mathscr{N}$icolas tried not to think about this morning throughout his whole ride around the nearby mountains. No matter what he did to distract himself; however, nothing worked. All he thought about was last night's conversation with Miss McLaren and waking up this morning having fallen asleep sitting next to her. If the whole thing wasn't a reminder enough, the ache in his neck only made it worse.

What was wrong with him, and what on earth was he thinking?

As he rode back to camp, a slight groan vibrated through his chest. He wasn't supposed to get involved like this, wasn't supposed to think about anything other than the mission at hand. And what had he done? He allowed a woman to captivate his thoughts and skew his mind.

How had he let it happen? And worse, why did he let it happen?

Because she's interesting, he thought to himself. *And beautiful. And she's got a charisma that makes me want to know more about her.*

He let out another groan and swung his leg over his saddle, climbing down from his horse before he walked it over to the tie line and tied the reins. The horse sneezed and shook its head, biting at the bit a few times before it lowered its head and ripped at the tall grass.

Nicolas loosened the girth and checked his rifle and saddle bags before making his way to the small camp he'd made for himself. He hadn't gone as far as to buy the same sort of wagon as the other travelers, instead opting for something small that would hold the minimal supplies he would need for the few weeks he would spend with the wagon train before turning back for Fort Boise. His one horse could also pull it without trouble.

With a deep breath, he lay down in the grass, stretching his legs out in front of him as he glanced around the camp. Although every inch of him wanted to look for Miss McLaren, he didn't allow himself to. Instead, he purposefully looked in every other direction, focusing on watching the different couples go about their daily chores.

"Mr. Kelly?" a voice asked behind him.

Nicolas sat up, turning toward the voice. "Mr. McLaren." He moved to stand, but the man held out his hand as though to tell him not to. "What can I do for you, Sir?"

"I was just coming over to ask yeh if yeh'd like to have supper with Charlotte and me this evening."

"Oh . . um . . ." For a moment, he thought of declining the invitation. Not because he wanted to be rude or didn't wish to have dinner with them, but because deep down, another evening spent in Miss McLaren's company would only distract him more.

"I know it's late in the day to be asking. But I see yeh haven't started to get yer supper ready, and we already have our stew on. Charlotte makes a mean stew, too. I promise yeh, yeh won't regret it."

Nicolas continued to fight against the word no, and while he wanted to say it, it got caught in his throat and wouldn't budge. "If you say so. I'd be glad to join you two."

"Perfect."

"Does Miss McLaren know you are over here?"

Mr. McLaren smiled, tucking his chin to his chest as he shook his head. "Aye, that would be a no. But she'll find out when yeh show up this evening."

~

*N*icolas's stomach fluttered as he made his way over to the McLaren's wagon. He saw Miss McLaren kneeling by the fire as she leaned over a pot, stirring its contents and smelling the steam. Her fire-red curls bounced with her movement, the color of the strands was bright and glistened as the sun began to set for the evening.

She looked up at him, furrowing her brow. "May I help yeh, Mr. Kelly?" she asked.

"Oh. Uh, your uncle invited me over for supper."

She cocked her head to the side, lifting one eyebrow as she leaned back and folded her arms across her chest. "Oh, did he, now? Well, isn't that . . . lovely."

Nicolas hooked his thumb over his shoulder. "I can leave if you want."

Although he said the words, he couldn't help but hope that she wouldn't take him up on it. He didn't want to leave any more than he didn't want to poke his own eyes out.

"No. No. It's all right with me. Stay if yeh want."

He pointed toward the pot hanging over the fire as he moved around the log and sat down. "It smells good. Whatever it is."

"It's just stew, Mr. Kelly." She chuckled as she waved her hand and turned her attention back to the pot.

"You know, you might as well call me Nicolas. No sense in being formal." His heart thumped as she looked at him.

"All right, then, Nicolas." She stuck her hand out to shake his. "I'm Charlotte."

"Well, Charlotte, it's nice to meet you."

She smiled and went back to the stew. "So, how long are yeh gonna be traveling with the wagon train?"

"I don't know. I thought perhaps until the Whitman Mission or The Dalles."

"That's quite a trek to make only to turn around and head back to Fort Boise."

"Well, I'm hoping that my luck will prevail and I find the man I'm searching for before then." He snorted and shrugged his shoulders.

"What is the man wanted for?"

"Several murders, spanning a few states."

Her brow furrowed, and her lips twitched. A sense of tension spread through her shoulders, and her hands fumbled with the spoon. She dropped it in the dirt.

"Oh, for the love . . ." A growl hinted through her hissed breath, and she fetched the spoon, dunking it into a nearby bucket of water before rubbing it with her hands to clean it.

"May I help you with anything?" he asked.

"No. I'm all right." Although she said the words, the tone in her voice said otherwise, but he didn't know if he should press the issue or let it go. "Do yeh think he's in the area?" she asked, keeping her gaze on the pot as she stirred the stew with a cleaned spoon.

"I don't know. I had word he was. I'll find him. I always do."

She glanced at him, and a half smile spread across her lips. "That's mighty confident of yeh."

"Well, I have years of experience in it, so I think I'm safe when I say I'll get him just like I've gotten the rest of them."

"And how many men have yeh gotten, Mr . . . Nicolas."

He sucked in a breath as his name rolled across her tongue. He'd never heard it said with such an accent and the sound of it made him smile on the inside. He didn't want to admit that he wanted to hear it more often.

"I think ten or twelve."

"So, yeh've been busy, then?"

"Quite."

The two of them exchanged glances, and she smiled again. Just as the night before, the time in her company seemed to ease his mind and calm his soul. There was something about their time together that whether they were talking or there was nothing but silence between them, it didn't matter. There was a peace to it, a comfort.

"Ah, Mr. Kelly." Mr. McLaren rounded the wagon, heaving a deep sigh. "Good to see yeh."

"It's good to see you. Thank you again for inviting me this evening."

"Of course. We've got to give yeh some of that good ole' Irish hospitality, now, don't we?" Mr. McLaren glanced between his niece and Nicolas. "I trust the lass over here has been welcoming."

"Aye, I have." Charlotte wiggled her eyebrows at her uncle, then furrowed them. "Even if yeh failed to mention yeh invited him for supper."

"Aye, yes, sorry, I forgot to mention it." Mr. McLaren tucked his chin, and although he tried to hide it, Nicolas saw a little smirk on the man's lips. It was as though he'd done it on purpose.

Exactly what was this man up to, Nicolas thought to himself.

"Well, it doesn't really matter now, does it?" Mr. McLaren said to Charlotte. "He's here, and we got enough stew. Might as well enjoy the night."

"Aye, might as well." Although she shot her uncle another glare, there was a hint of amusement as though she wasn't annoyed, but she still wanted to give her uncle a hard time about it anyway.

Her uncle smiled and winked, then moved to another water bucket, fetching a ladle from it and taking a drink.

"So, Mr. Kelly," he said, moving to where Nicolas sat, sitting next to him. "When did yeh decide to become a Pinkerton?"

Nicolas sucked in a breath again. "I think I was about ten years old."

Mr. McLaren blinked, and his head jerked. "Ten? Wow. That's quite a young age for a lad to know what he wants to do in life, and especially such a dangerous but commendable profession. What was it that made up yer mind?"

"I was witness to something."

The niece and uncle both glanced at him.

"What was it?" Charlotte asked.

Nicolas hesitated. While he never minded sharing the incident in the alleyway, there was something about sharing it with a woman. It didn't seem right. It didn't seem proper.

He cleared his throat. "Two men were . . . harassing a young woman, and I stopped it. Watching the doctor tend to the woman . . . well, I just made a choice right then and there that I would make sure criminals would do their time and wouldn't be around to do it again."

Charlotte raised one eyebrow. "It sounds like there's more to the story that yeh aren't saying."

"And for a good reason." Nicolas laughed, hoping the gesture would give her a hint that the story wasn't for her ears.

"And what reason is that?" While her eyebrow was still raised, she wiggled it, cocking her head to the side.

She was not making this easy, he thought to himself. Although, I suppose that's her and just one of the reasons she was so intriguing.

"I don't think it's a proper story for a woman to hear."

She snorted. "I can assure yeh, Nicolas; there isn't anything yeh could say that I haven't heard about or seen in my life. Especially growing up with that man right over there." She pointed to her uncle.

"And just what is that supposed to mean, Lass?" Mr.

McLaren straightened his shoulders, brushing his hand against his chest. Although another in his situation would probably have gotten annoyed or defensive, Mr. McLaren only seemed amused at his niece. As though it had been a running joke between them about the way he had brought her up in the world. "I'll have yeh know that I never did anything that was illegal." A slight chuckle vibrated through his chest. "Ungrateful little Lass. I'll have yeh know I worked hard after yer father . . ."

"Aye. Yeh did." Charlotte gave him a smirk. "Yeh know I love yeh, but it probably wasn't the best idea to take me around with yeh when yeh made yer sales."

"I'll give yeh that." Mr. McLaren laughed. "Although, I only took yeh because no one ever said no to me when I had yeh with me. It was like they knew I was just trying to make ends meet so I could take care of yeh."

"And now the truth comes out." She chuckled.

"What did you sell?" Nicolas asked.

"Anything I could get my hands on. Someone once called me a Rag Picker. I suppose that's what they called men like me. Someone who hunted through trash for items that could be sold and used again." Mr. McLaren heaved a deep sigh. "I'll admit that it probably wasn't the most upstanding of jobs, but it put food on the table, and that's all that matters."

"Sounds like it."

"I never did anything illegal. I made sure of that. But after my brother . . . times were tough."

Nicolas wanted to ask about Charlotte's father, given it was the second time the two of them mentioned him, and it sounded as though he wasn't alive anymore. But he also didn't want to be rude or ask them any questions they didn't want to answer. Especially when they didn't elaborate on the subject without him asking, he got the impression it wasn't a subject either of them wished to broach.

"Still, though, there were times I shouldn't have taken a lass.

I know that now. Of course, she wouldn't be the strong woman she is now." Mr. McLaren smiled, almost beaming as he looked at his niece. "Tough as nails, that one is, Mr. Kelly. Yeh won't find another lass like her anywhere. No matter how hard yeh try."

Nicolas looked at Charlotte, remembering how he met her in the mountains shooting at targets in the trees. "I don't doubt it," he said.

Charlotte glanced down at the ground, tucking her hair behind one ear before meeting his gaze. He didn't want to admit that while he shouldn't think of her in any other way other than another woman on a wagon train that he would soon part from and never see again, deep down, he knew there was nothing else he wanted more than her.

Not even the chance at finding Mr. Jack Carter.

EIGHT

CHARLOTTE

Charlotte scrubbed the pot from the stew as the night before replayed in her mind. She hadn't wanted to think about how wonderful it had been to be in Nicolas's company again or how much fun it was, and yet, she also didn't want to deny it any longer. A bitter battle had raged inside her heart and mind, and for the first time, one side—the one she hadn't considered—was winning. Why couldn't she seek out Mr. Carter, do as she wanted, then think about a life of love, marriage, and family after?

The fact was, she could.

And she would.

"Hello, Mr. Kelly," her uncle said behind her, and as she glanced over her shoulder, she saw the Pinkerton approach their wagon, leading his horse.

"I told you last night; you're more than welcome to call me Nicolas."

The two men shook hands.

"Aye, I know. Still seems odd for some reason. But I will try." Uncle Ned ran a hand through his hair. "What can I do for yeh this fine morning?"

Nicolas glanced at Charlotte. "Well, I was about to go hunting to see if I can get some meat before we leave camp and get back on the trail, and I was wondering if Charlotte wanted to go with me. It might give her another chance to work on her shooting skills." He chuckled, shaking his head as though to correct a mistake he knew he had made. "Not to say that she needs work. But even I need to keep my skills honed."

"Aye. Aye. I believe one should keep using the skills God gives them." Uncle Ned pointed toward her. "Yer more than welcome to ask her if she would like to go."

Nicolas moved toward her, smiling at her. "Would you like to go?"

Of course, she wanted to scream yes, jumping to her feet before she could even blink. But while that part of her nearly exploded with the freedom, the other part corralled her gut reaction. She stood slowly, squinting from the early morning sunlight as she looked at him. She lifted her hand to shield her eyes.

"I suppose I could go," she said, trying to keep her voice calm as she hid the burst of excitement in her chest. "I'll get my things."

"And I'll tack up the horse," Ned added, giving them both a broad grin as he tipped his hat.

She didn't know whether to laugh at him or be embarrassed.

～

Charlotte crept through the trees behind Nicolas. He paused every few steps, looking in all directions as though he was searching for a sign of anything they could hunt. After a few silent seconds, he would lift his hand, wiggling his fingers for her to continue following him.

"I don't think there is anything around here," he finally whispered.

"Maybe we should stop for a bit and wait."

He looked around, furrowing his brow before nodding. "Yeah. We can do that." He pointed toward a large fallen tree. "We can hide in that thicket over there behind the log."

"All right."

They made their way over to the log, and Nicolas held out his hand. She looked at it for a moment, then grabbed it as she climbed over the log one leg at a time. The warmth of his palm against hers sent heat up the back of her neck, and her cheeks flushed.

"Thank yeh."

"You're welcome."

They nestled down in the small clearing, and as he laid his gun on the tree, she set hers down on the ground.

"How long do yeh think we should wait?" she asked.

He glanced around the trees and sky. "For a bit. I know there are several herds of deer in the area. I've seen them while riding in these mountains."

"Well, that's a good sign."

"Have you ever hunted before?" he asked, adjusting his seat on the ground before stretching his back and shoulders.

"Honestly?" Another wave of heat rushed up the back of her neck. "No, I haven't."

"Is there a reason you haven't?"

She shook her head. "Just haven't had the chance, is all. But I've wanted to."

"Well, I guess you're going to get your chance today. Or I should say I hope so." He glanced around them again, then up at the sky. "I like to get out before the sun comes up. That's usually the best time."

"Why didn't yeh go this morning, then?" she asked.

He shrugged. "Not sure. I guess it was a last-minute choice to go at all. I think it will be all right. And even if we don't get anything, it's fun just going for the ride."

"That's true."

"I enjoyed your stew last night. It was good."

"Yeah, yeh said that. Several times while yeh were eating it and after."

"What can I say? When I like something, I say it." He chuckled.

"May I ask yeh something?" she asked, glancing at him. Her heart thumped as their gazes met. Although she'd noticed his eyes when they first met, there was something about the morning light that brightened the green hue, and she knew if she stared at them much longer, she wouldn't be able to speak.

"Of course."

"What was that story you didn't want to tell? The one about the woman who, in helping her, made you decide to become a Pinkerton?"

He inhaled a deep breath, letting it out slowly. "Ah. That."

"Yeah. That."

"I think I was about ten. Not yet a man, but close enough. My parents had been on my backside night and day about finding a place in this world. I didn't want to work at the sawmill like my older brother, and I didn't want to work on a nearby ranch like my younger brother. I knew I wanted something else out of this life, but I just didn't know what."

"I can understand that."

"I was walking around the city, kicking rocks down the cobblestone, trying to figure out life, when I heard a woman crying. By the time I got there, they had already ripped her clothes and had their way . . ." Nicolas inhaled another deep breath. "They'd beaten her. She was bleeding, crying, and they were standing over her, trying to decide what to do with her—the evidence, as they called her."

"What did yeh do?"

He snorted. "I grabbed a board that was leaning up against several stacked crates. I may have been outnumbered two to one, but when you have a weapon like a big chunk of wood . . ." He snorted again. "I knocked them both out before running back down to the street and shouting for help. They went to jail, of course, so there was some justice. But I don't think it was enough for the woman."

"I would doubt that was too."

"It was then I knew I wanted to help people by putting criminals behind bars."

"It's a commendable thing to do."

He shrugged. "I don't do it for the notoriety."

"I know. I wasn't trying to say that yeh did."

"I know." He reached out, laying his hand on her shoulder. She glanced over at his hand, and heat flushed her cheeks. He pulled his hand away. "I'm sorry. I didn't mean to . . . do that."

"It's all right."

Silence fell between them, and Charlotte's heartbeat kicked up. While it was still a calm silence, there was something about it that felt different. It wasn't the same as it was the first night they'd spent together under the stars near the fire. It wasn't a bad difference, but it was different.

"You know, I don't think I told you before; I enjoyed the company last night. Your uncle . . ." Nicolas let his voice trail off as his eyes unfocused in a distracted haze.

"I know what yeh mean." A slight snort left her nose as she pictured Nicolas laughing with Uncle Ned. It had been a long time since she'd seen such mirth in her uncle, and she hadn't known how much she missed it until last night. Although she knew the death of her pa—his brother—had affected him, she hadn't known exactly how much.

Of course, some might think such was expected, given she was going through her own grief. Still, normal or not, she wanted to be the niece that saw her uncle's struggles just as much as she saw her own. She didn't want to be selfish.

"I think it was good for him. Laughing like that again. He needed it."

Nicolas stared at her for a moment, and his brow furrowed, then softened. "May I ask you something?"

"I suppose it depends on what it is." She gave him a half smile.

"He mentioned your father and taking care of you. I was just wondering what he meant." Nicolas paused. "If you don't wish to tell me, I understand."

"No, no. It's all right. My uncle raised me after my pa died when I was just five years old. I would never complain about my childhood or growing up with him. He was the best, and he did everything he could. He just wasn't my pa."

"I can understand that. May I ask what happened to your father?"

She glanced down at the ground as heat rushed up the back of her neck. A lump formed in her throat, and although she tried to swallow it, it wouldn't budge.

"He . . . he was murdered."

Nicolas's eyes widened, and he blinked several times as his head jerked slightly backward. "I . . . I'm sorry. If I'd known . . . I wouldn't have asked."

"It's all right that yeh did. I don't speak of it much, but if asked, I'll tell yeh."

"Do you know what happened?"

"I saw it."

Nicolas's head jerked again, and his mouth fell open. "You saw it?"

"We were at the county fair. He was talking to another man about money the man owed him. I later found out it was a business deal he'd made. The man didn't have the money, and words were exchanged. The man drew a gun and . . ." She let her voice trail off, not wanting to relive the memories any more than she already did in her nightmares.

"Was the man ever caught?"

She shook her head, and Nicolas closed his eyes as he exhaled a deep breath.

"I'm sorry."

Charlotte looked at the man sitting next to her, thinking that if anyone in this world would understand her need for justice, he would. How could he not? When he, himself, chose the profession he did because of a woman who was wronged and because someone had taken something from her that she could never get back.

"I have to admit that I've been searching for the man ever since."

"What are you planning to do if you find him?"

She shrugged, hesitating to tell him. "I don't know. Perhaps seek the justice I was never given."

Nicolas's brow furrowed, and his eyes narrowed for a moment. His face seemed to harden. "Why would you want to do that yourself?"

"Why would I not? None was given to me."

"That should be something that a sheriff does or even a man like me. Not you."

"I don't see it that way since the sheriff did nothing."

His eyes narrowed again. "You should."

A flicker of annoyance burned in her chest, and she closed her eyes, shaking her head. "I don't believe yeh have a say in the matter, Mr. Kelly."

"I do since I'm the law."

All of the breath was kicked from her lungs with his six words. While they hadn't meant much to her before, now they held a meaning she couldn't ignore no matter how much she wanted to. She'd been so foolish to tell him what she did. She should never have.

"What are you planning to do?" he asked.

She shrugged, trying to ignore his question.

"You shouldn't do whatever it is you don't want to tell me. You shouldn't do anything at all. You should leave the situation alone."

She shook her head again, blowing out a breath. "What *I should do* is return to the camp." She stood, and a couple of rabbits hiding in the bushes nearby fled their hiding spot.

"Charlotte, wait." Nicolas stood too. "Let's talk about this. What are you planning to do?"

"I'm not going to tell yeh." She glanced over her shoulder, hissing her words. "Just forget I said anything."

"Charlotte. Charlotte!"

No matter how often he called after her, she never looked back. She couldn't believe she'd let herself believe that telling him anything was a good thing. She also couldn't believe she'd ever thought she should think about love, marriage, or anything other than what she'd always thought about—getting justice and revenge against Mr. Carter.

NINE

CHARLOTTE

Charlotte rode back into the camp, barely halting her horse before she threw her leg over the saddle and dismounted. Her boots hit the ground, and she jerked the reins over the horse's head, leading it back to the tie line. A slight growl vibrated through her chest. She hadn't wanted to give Mr. Kelly the satisfaction of knowing that she'd thought about what he'd said to her the whole ride back to camp, but unfortunately, that was just what she'd done.

With every step her horse took his words repeated inside her head, building upon one another each time until her simmering annoyance turned into a raging forest fire of anger.

How dare he say what he did. How dare he tell her it's not her place to seek the justice she did. Did she not have a say? Did she not have the right to not only her feelings but to act upon those feelings?

"How was the hunt?" Uncle Ned rounded the back of the wagon. A broad smile spread across his face.

She flashed him a glare. "I wish I'd never gone. Remind me never to speak to that man again."

Uncle Ned's smile vanished. "What happened?"

"I don't want to talk about it."

She stormed down to the river, stomping until she reached the water, where she stopped, shoved her hands onto her hips, and let out a scream. She didn't mean to shout as loud as she did, but she also couldn't deny how it had made her feel a little better, even if it was for only a moment.

"Charlotte?" a voice asked behind her.

She spun to find Emma and Abby kneeling in front of the water several feet away. In her haste, she hadn't noticed anyone else near the river, and looking upon their wide eyes and gaped mouths, a tickle of embarrassment warmed through her chest. She hadn't meant for anyone to see her outburst.

"Are you all right?" Emma asked,

While part of her wanted to say yes, the other part—the one who wished to share the audacity and ridiculousness of what Mr. Kelly had said to her—pushed her to say no.

"It's that annoying Mr. Kelly."

"The Pinkerton? I thought he . . . and you . . ."

Charlotte laughed. "Not even if he was the last man on this earth. I can't believe I listened to yeh about him. He is the worst sort of man."

The two women glanced at one another.

"What did he do?" Abby asked.

"He told me he was the law and I shouldn't have a say in what happens to the man who killed my pa."

The two women glanced at one another again, and while Abby inhaled a deep breath, Emma closed her eyes for a moment.

Charlotte cocked her head to the side. She'd seen that moment when others had opinions they either didn't want to share or didn't know if they should share.

"What is it?" she asked them.

Emma bit her lip, closing her eyes for a second again as she held out her hands. "Don't be angry . . . but . . . perhaps he's right. Not in that you don't have a say, but in that he's the law. Perhaps he should be the one to seek justice for you."

"The law did nothing when my pa was murdered. It's not going to do anything now, all these years later. No one will help me. No one wants to help me."

"Maybe he will and does. He seems fond of you. Perhaps once he finds the man he's looking for, he will search for the man you are looking for. Perhaps he will find him and bring him to justice. Shouldn't you give him a chance?"

"A chance? Yeh want me to give him a chance?" Her Irish accent deepened in her anger, and her eye twitched with the stress of the heat pulsing through her body. "Why must everyone tell me what I should or shouldn't do? Especially when they have never lived a day of my life. Yeh don't know what it's like to watch a man murder yer father, so don't tell me what I should do."

"You're right. I haven't, and I didn't mean to offend you or make you think I'm telling you what to do. Everything I've said was only a suggestion."

"Well, stop suggesting things. Just . . . just stop talking at all." While Charlotte didn't mean to shout, she also didn't care when her voice rose.

She was done being told what and what not to do.

She was done being told what she should and shouldn't feel.

She was done with everyone saying anything to her.

She was going to find Mr. Carter and get the justice she deserved. No one would stop her. No one.

≈

NICOLAS

*N*icolas galloped back to the camp, stopping as he reached the tie line. He swung his leg over and climbed down, tying the reins to the line. He secured his rifle, and as he made his way over to Charlotte's wagon, Mr. McLaren approached him, holding out his hands.

"I don't know what yeh said to her, Lad, but if I were yeh, I wouldn't try to talk to her right now."

"But I want to explain."

"I know yeh do. But it's no good. Not right now. She's too upset to listen to yeh." Mr. McLaren shook his head, heaving a deep sigh. "She's too upset to talk to anyone. Even I couldn't get through to her if I tried."

"I didn't mean for any of this to happen."

"I know yeh didn't." Her uncle shook his head. "May I ask what happened though? Charlotte wouldn't tell me."

"She told me about her father and . . . what happened."

"Aye. It was an awful time. She was so young, and of course, I wasn't the best substitute. The Lord knows I tried to care for the lass as I would my own. But I wasn't a father, and I wasn't her father. I knew nothing of raising a daughter."

"She said you were wonderful, and you did the best you could."

"But what is the best when yeh know nothing? Seems to me like it's just mediocre at best."

"That's not what I got from what she said. I doubt she would ever call you mediocre." Nicolas reached out and laid his hand on Charlotte's uncle's shoulder. "You did a great job raising her, and she loves you so much."

"Well, I love her that much. Perhaps even more. She's grown into a fine lady, and I'm so proud." Mr. McLaren's eyes unfocused slightly as though he was reliving memories, and although he seemed to get lost in them, after just a moment, his face changed, and he raised one eyebrow. "But still, that doesn't explain what happened."

"After she told me about her father, she also told me about the man who murdered him."

"Aye. She told yeh about him, did she?"

"Yes, she did. And after she did, she mentioned looking for him. I'm afraid I may have overstepped by sharing my opinion of her doing that. I think that should be left to the sheriff or my office. She didn't seem to share my opinion."

"No, I don't think she would." Mr. McLaren shook his head and heaved a deep sigh. "The sheriff wasn't too keen on helping her after the murder nor any of the years since."

"Do you know why?"

"Nah. I never found out, and even though I asked, my questions were never answered."

While Nicolas never wanted to believe that a man who could wear a badge that said he would protect people would neglect his duty, he also knew how Irish immigrants were often seen. At least how they were in the bigger cities, often looked at as people who brought disease and death, there were certain groups who blamed the Irish.

Should the sheriff in question feel like some of the men, he knew about the Irish . . . well, he could see how Charlotte's father's case would be shoved aside.

"Well, no matter what was done in the past, that doesn't mean I can't take up the case now."

"Did yeh tell Charlotte that?"

"I told her that finding this man should be done by the law."

"So yeh told her what I've been saying all these years. Not to mention what her friends have been saying."

"I suppose I did."

"And let me guess . . . she didn't take too kindly to the advice."

Nicholas inhaled a deep breath, closing his eyes for a second. "No, she did not."

"One thing yeh need to know about Charlotte is she's never one to do as others say. Especially when it's something she doesn't want to hear."

Nicolas snorted. "Yeah, I got that impression. I have to say it was one of the things that piqued my interest in her. She's out to forge her own path, and that's rare in most women. I admire it."

"Aye, I admire it too. But I also think she can be a little too headstrong for her own good." Mr. McLaren exhaled a deep sigh as he tucked his chin to his chest and grabbed the bridge of his nose. "I've told her so many times. Just forget him. Forget about Mr. Carter and get on with yer life. Find a man, fall in love, have a family."

Nicolas's brow furrowed. "I beg your pardon? Mister who?"

"Mr. Carter. Jim . . . Jacob . . . I can't remember."

"Jack?"

"Aye. That's it. Mr. Jack Carter."

Nicolas sucked in a breath. "That's the man I'm looking for."

TEN

CHARLOTTE

Charlotte sat in front of the fire, and as the flames licked at the chunk of wood in the middle, she took the knife blade in her hand to the stick in her hand. She carved the stick's end into a point, slicing away until the tip was sharp.

"I think yeh got it good enough, don't yeh?" Uncle Ned sat down next to her, motioning toward the stick.

"Depends," she said dryly.

"On?"

"On where I want to stick it." Her jaw clenched as she hissed her words.

He blinked a couple of times and inhaled a deep breath. "I guess that's understandable. Have yeh spoken to Mr. Kelly?"

"No." She glanced at her uncle. "And don't think I'm gonna just because yeh think I should."

He opened his mouth but closed it, letting out a hmm noise as he furrowed his brow.

"Really, Uncle?" She glanced at him again with a slight growl to her voice. "So, yeh are planning on telling me that I should talk to him?"

"Well, I have to say yes, but—"

"Are yeh bloody serious?" Her voice rose.

He held his hands up. "Just hear me out before yeh come at me, all right?"

"And why should I do that?"

"Because Mr. Kelly is hunting Mr. Carter."

Her uncle's words were like a punch to the gut, and as she sucked in a breath, her spit choked her, and she coughed and sputtered.

"What did yeh say?" she asked her uncle after her coughing fit.

"The man he's looking for . . . it's the same man you're looking for. Mr. Jack Carter."

"How do yeh know?"

"He told me." Uncle Ned heaved a deep sigh. "He felt bad after yer conversation and wants to apologize to yeh."

Questions fired off in her mind, and she struggled with all of them. Everything her uncle was saying all seemed to blend into this mess of incoherent words that her mind couldn't make sense of.

"He didn't mean to upset yeh, Charlotte. I think . . . I think hearing about what yeh wanted to do . . . I think it scared him. I think the thought of yeh going up against a man like Mr. Carter scared him too."

"I can handle meself."

"I know yeh can. And I think Mr. Kelly knows yeh can too, deep down anyway. But even knowing what we do, we still fear the notion of what yer doing. I know I don't want anything happening to yeh."

While so much of Charlotte wanted to tell her uncle there wasn't anything to worry about, she also couldn't deny she had her own concerns. Who wouldn't when they thought of taking on a dangerous man? She didn't want to think that she could lose against him. She'd doubted herself far too many times in her life, and she didn't want to do it anymore, even if the pesky thoughts tried to cross her mind every so often.

No, she thought. I'm not going to do it now.

"Nothing is gonna happen, Uncle."

"Yeh don't know that, Lass. Yeh can think it, but no one knows what tomorrow will bring, and yeh, certainly, can't predict the future."

"It's not about predicting anything. It's about what I'm capable of." A tiny hint of anger simmered in her chest. She didn't need anyone else telling her what to feel or what to do. She didn't need anyone else trying to cast their own doubts upon her as though they were doing so out of kindness. She stood and threw down the stick she'd been carving.

"Where are yeh going?"

"I need to take a walk."

Before her uncle could say another word, she strode off toward the horses on the tie line. Far too many thoughts and questions swam around her mind, and although she knew she needed to give each one of them attention, she knew she couldn't. At least not now.

She found one of their horses on the end of the tie line, happily ripping grass and chewing it. It swished its tail at the flies bugging it, shaking its head a few times as its ears swiveled from front to back. She ran her hand down its back, letting her fingers separate the fine, light tan hairs. Chestnut is what the rancher who had sold them the horse called it; this gelding had been her favorite of the four they'd purchased for the trip. The horse flicked his tail several more times and kept eating, only lifting his head every few bites to chew the grass in his mouth before taking even more bites.

For a moment, she wished she could be as content as the horse whose only concern at the moment was food and stuffing as much of it into its belly as possible. She snorted a slight laugh at the thought. Of course, life wasn't easy for the horses on the wagon train. Life is never easy for anyone, and the long days of pulling wagons across the countryside worked their bodies to the bone. However, watching the horse now while it enjoyed the peace of a good meal, she couldn't help but feel envious.

Jealous of a horse, she thought with another snorted laugh. *I can't believe my life has come to that.*

She glanced over the camp, noticing two horses and riders galloping toward them. Other travelers noticed them too, and as the two men on horseback neared the wagons, they slowed their horses to a trot and then to a walk. William and Abby were the first to greet them, and after talking to the two men for a moment, William turned and pointed toward the direction of Mr. Kelly's camp.

Intrigued with the newcomers, Charlotte watched as they made their way over to Mr. Kelly, giving him a wave as they approached.

What on earth is going on, she thought.

She watched the two men as she hid behind the chestnut gelding. The two climbed down from their horses, and while one grabbed and held both sets of reins, the other reached into his pocket and yanked out a folded piece of paper. He unfolded it, pointing to whatever was printed on it before handing it to Mr. Kelly.

Even more, interest piqued in Charlotte's chest, and she watched the three men as Mr. Kelly studied the piece of paper. He turned and pointed toward his horses on the tie line, and he, along with the two men, began to make their way over.

Charlotte's heart thumped, and she knelt in the grass, hiding behind her horse.

"Did you see him with your own eyes, or were you told he was in the area?" Mr. Kelly asked. His voice trailed over the horses even if Charlotte couldn't see him.

"Sort of both. We heard he was in the area first, and then we came across him hiding out in an old cabin not too far from here. I thought to engage, but I knew you'd want to handle it yourself, seeing as how my son nor myself is the law. We are just farmers."

"No, you're right. I do, and there's no need for you to get wrapped up in this mess. Not to mention, Jack Carter is a dangerous man. He's wanted for several murders. I wouldn't want you and your family to be added to the list." Mr. Kelly paused, heaving a deep breath. "Can you tell me where the cabin is?"

"Yes, Sir. It's about five miles north of here. If you follow the river, you'll run right into it."

Charlotte glanced over at the riverbank. Her heartbeat kicked up again and a lump formed in her throat.

Follow the river, and yeh'll run right into it, she thought. *Follow the river.*

She peeked at the two men through the horse's legs, watching Mr. Kelly shove the piece of paper back into his pocket and slap the man on the back of the shoulder. "Thank you for your help. I'll see to it that you are given the reward for helping find him."

The man held up his hands and shook his head, ducking his chin for a moment. "Knowing we helped is reward enough. I want to help get him behind bars, especially if he's wanted for murder. I know how I would feel if he'd done away with one of my own."

"Still, the money will be nice for you and your family," Mr. Kelly laughed. "So, I will personally see that you receive it."

As they walked off, the two men continued talking while they headed back toward Mr. Kelly's wagon and campsite. The man's son watched the two men as Charlotte did, and as soon as the men were out of earshot, she stood and grabbed the saddle lying in the grass near her horse. It was in the same place she'd dumped it that morning after returning from the hunting fiasco with Mr. Kelly.

She threw on the blanket and saddle, and her hands trembled as she tightened the cinch around the horse's belly. She knew it was only a matter of time before Mr. Kelly would head out looking for Mr. Carter, and she would have to leave now if she wanted her chance at the man responsible for her father's death.

After putting the bit in the horse's mouth and sliding the bridle over its ears, she pulled it away from the tie line and stuck her foot in the stirrup. With a few bounces, she hoisted herself onto the horse, swung her leg over, and cued the animal into a trot and then a gallop, not even looking over her shoulder as she headed toward the river.

And headed north.

ELEVEN

NICOLAS

*A*fter seeing the father and son off, Nicolas heaved a deep sigh. He'd been looking for a break in this case, and while he knew he would find one, he hadn't known when. He didn't want to admit that he'd even been concerned that he wouldn't find Mr. Carter for a while. It had already been nearly two years since he started his search for the man. He didn't want to think about it taking another two years or more.

He inhaled another deep breath and glanced over at Charlotte's wagon. He knew he needed to tell her, but so much of him told him he should think about it first. He didn't know if he wanted her to know because he didn't know if she would try something stupid, something he didn't want her to do. At the same time, a twinge of guilt prickled in his chest at the thought of not telling her.

She deserved to know.

Didn't she?

Mr. Carter killed her father.

And the man took everything from her. Her father. Her childhood. Her hopes. Her dreams. Sure Nicolas hadn't seen his parents in more years than he could count, but he'd written them. They knew of his whereabouts, and he knew of theirs. He knew they were safe and they were happy just living their lives on their farm in Iowa, tending to the cattle and the garden just as they had every day of every year he'd lived with them.

She never had any of that.

Instead, she buried her father when she was just a little girl.

She deserves to know, he thought.

With a deep, inhaled breath, he adjusted the waistband of his pants and made his way over to Charlotte's wagon. He wasn't sure exactly what he wanted to say, but he hoped that when he saw her, he would know.

"Or at least have an idea," he said to himself.

Mr. McLaren glanced up from tending to the fire as Nicolas approached.

"Good afternoon," Mr. McLaren said, nodding.

"Afternoon."

Mr. McLaren glanced over his shoulder toward the direction the father and son had left. "Friends of yers?" His Irish accent reminded Nicolas of Charlotte's.

"They came with news."

"What kind of news?"

"The kind I've been waiting for. It seems that some other Pinkertons were in the area and were asking around about Mr. Carter. They came across a farmer and his son who had seen Mr. Carter just a few days ago in a rundown cabin not far from here."

"Aye, they did, did they? Well, that's interesting." Mr. McLaren hesitated on each word, uttering the syllables slowly as though he wanted to think about every single one before he actually said them.

"I thought you and Charlotte should know."

"Well, that's kind of yeh."

"Is she around?" Nicolas glanced at the wagon's wheels, hoping to see her shoes peeking around the bottom as though she was standing on the other side, listening to their conversation.

"I'm afraid she's not."

"What do you mean? Where did she go?"

Mr. McLaren inhaled a deep breath, letting his cheeks puff up before blowing the air out slowly. He looked as though he had something he knew he should say, but it was also something he didn't want to say.

"I don't know where she went. I told her about what yeh had told me, and she didn't . . . well, she didn't take it well. She got angry and left."

"But she couldn't have gone far. It's not as though she could be hiding." Nicolas chuckled at his own joke. He knew the situation wasn't funny, but he also knew if he didn't make himself laugh—even if it was a little—right now, his concerned thoughts about where she was would take control of his mind. "Perhaps she went to speak with one of her friends."

"Perhaps."

~

"I'm sorry, Mr. Kelly, but I haven't seen her," Mrs. Campbell glanced at Mrs. Garrison, and the latter shook her head, agreeing with her friend. Nicolas didn't want to admit how hearing this news sent his mind through another wave of panic. He didn't want to assume anything, but he also couldn't deny his growing concern over the situation.

Had she run off into the nearby mountains to calm herself?

"Have you asked Mrs. Ford?" Mrs. Campbell asked.

"No, not yet."

Nicolas followed the two women to another wagon, finding Mr. and Mrs. Ford sitting near a fire.

"Have either of you seen Charlotte?" Mrs. Garrison asked.

Mr. Ford shook his head and glanced at his wife. While

Nicholas suspected finding the same reaction in Mrs. Ford, he was surprised to see her bite her lip and avert her gaze to the ground.

"Lillian?" Mrs. Garrison asked, her voice deepening like a mother asking a child a question while knowing the child didn't want to answer it for fear of getting into trouble. "What do you know?"

"Nothing. I know nothing. I just saw her ride off. She looked as though she was in a hurry, but I don't know where she was going."

"Where was she headed?"

"Toward the river. She was heading that way."

Nicolas's heart sank as Mrs. Ford pointed not only toward the river but north, too.

Had she overheard his conversation with the father and son? Did she know about Mr. Carter's whereabouts? He tried to imagine walking toward his horse on the tie line, picturing if he'd seen anyone else standing near the horses. He couldn't see anything other than his own horse and how he'd only taken the father over there so no one could hear what they were speaking about.

He'd been so careless.

He should have checked.

Nicolas sucked in a breath. "What do you all know of her plans for Mr. Carter?"

All three women's eyes widened, and Mrs. Ford slapped her hand across her mouth.

"How do you know about Mr. Carter?" Mrs. Garrison asked. She blinked several times and inhaled a deep breath.

"Because he's the man I'm looking for."

Mrs. Garrison and Mrs. Campbell joined Mrs. Ford in covering their mouths with their hands. Mrs. Ford even let out a squeak, and all three women blinked at Nicolas. The pieces had already begun to fit into the puzzle, and Nicolas knew there was nothing else to do but to go after her.

He just hoped and prayed that he wasn't too late.

"Thank you for your help." He spun on his heel.

"Where are you going?" Mrs. Garrison said, running after him a few steps.

He glanced over his shoulder. "I think she went after him," he said. "And now I've got to find him before she does . . . and I've got to find her."

TWELVE

CHARLOTTE

*C*harlotte brushed a branch away from her view, peering down at the cabin in the middle of a clearing. The log structure sat near the river and had smoke coming from the chimney. She watched as the haze filtered into the trees, obscuring the leaves fluttering in the slight breeze. Her heart thumped.

Had she found the right cabin? Was the man she was looking for inside?

She'd dreamed of this moment for more years than she could count, and while the chance was suddenly upon her, she couldn't help but hesitate. Looking down at the cabin, her mind drifted to her uncle, and she replayed all the conversations they shared. Behind everything he'd ever said to her, there was fear and worry, and even though he always told her she could do anything she wanted, she knew there was a lie between the words. He didn't want her to go after Mr. Carter any more than any parent would want their child in harm's way.

For the first time in her quest, she wondered if she'd been thinking so much about her pa and her revenge that she forgot about everyone else.

For so many years, she'd thought of nothing else, and in the last few days, that had changed. A new world of possibilities had opened up, leaving her reeling.

Her horse ripped at a patch of grass behind her, and the noise caused her to flinch. She glanced over her shoulder, watching the animal chew, then take another bite, struggling with the bit in its mouth. The sudden distraction caused her, just for a second, to think of climbing back in the saddle and returning to camp.

No, she thought, shaking her head. *I'm here for a reason.*

As if to read her thoughts, a man opened the cabin's front door and stepped out onto the porch. He inhaled a deep breath and glanced around the yard, studying the trees around the house and the river and riverbank. He paused on a rather large boulder, lifting his hand to shield his eyes from the nearly setting sun as though he saw something or thought he did. Besides Charlotte, the only living things around him were a few birds in the trees and a bunny that hopped around the back of the cabin—unbeknownst to him.

Charlotte sucked in a breath.

Although she felt the tug to leave, she also felt the tug to stay.

Stay and finish what she'd always planned to do.

Her heart thumped, and she stood from crouching behind the bushes, turning toward her horse. She grabbed the reins, leading the horse out into a clearing to climb back in the saddle. The smooth leather hugged her body, and it creaked as she cued the horse across the river. Its hooves splashed in the water, drawing Mr. Carter's attention, and he blinked at her as she approached the cabin.

His eyes narrowed at first, but as he took in the look of her— a woman headed toward him—his body seemed to relax, and he smiled. She hadn't seen the likes of this man since she was just a little girl in that alleyway, and yet even in all that time, she hadn't forgotten him. Even if the years had aged him, he still looked the same with an oval-shaped face, tiny eyes that were too close together, and a crooked smile.

"Good afternoon, ma'am," he said. His voice had aged and deepened like the rest of him, but there was still the same pitch to it that ran cold through her veins. Although she'd thought about the sound of it, she hadn't thought about how it would make her feel.

"Good afternoon," she said dryly.

"Didn't know there was anyone riding around in these parts." He glanced around them as he lifted his hand and scratched the back of his neck. "Are you alone, or are you riding with someone else?"

For a moment, she thought of lying to him and telling him she wasn't alone. But what would be the point of it? It wasn't like she was scared for her life. While she didn't want to leave her uncle alone in this world nor turn her back on any dreams she'd imagined in the last few days, seeing the man standing in front of her had only made her hunger for justice more. What did it matter if Mr. Carter knew she was alone or not? It wouldn't change the reason she was here.

It wouldn't change anything.

"I'm alone," she said.

Mr. Carter blinked, and his head jerked slightly. His brow furrowed for a second as he chewed on the side of his lip. "Well, you're more than welcome to stay here for the night. If you need a place, that is."

"I don't."

"Oh. Well, if you want a meal, I think I can scrounge up some food. Do you like to eat rabbit?"

"Why are yeh offering me things?" she asked, cocking her head to the side.

He blinked at her again. "Well, I just thought . . . a woman, traveling alone . . . well, it just doesn't make any sense. Not out here."

"My wagon train isn't that far from here. I was just out riding when I came across the cabin."

Mr. Carter looked across the river and then scratched his chin. "A wagon train, huh?"

Charlotte studied the man for a moment as his voice trailed off. It was as though he became lost in his thoughts, and while she never wanted to assume what those thoughts were, she could imagine him thinking about whether or not he could rob the wagon train.

"Does that interest yeh?" she asked.

His head jerked, and he blinked at her. "Interest me? What's that supposed to mean?"

"Well, yeh just seemed like yeh were thinking about something, and I wondered what it was. Does it interest yeh that there is a wagon train close?"

He shrugged. "I don't know if I'd say that. I mean, I guess there have been other wagon trains in these parts since it's the road to Oregon. But what would I need of one when I got my place?" He hooked his thumb over his shoulder, pointing at the cabin.

"Yer place?" She looked over the rundown shack of a home with its broken windows and the roof caved in, in the corner. The place looked like it had been abandoned years ago and was now only a place of refuge for criminals passing through. "So, this is yer place?"

"I said it was, didn't I?" A slight hint of annoyance piqued in Mr. Carter's tone, and he furrowed his brow for a moment. "Anyway, what are you doing here if you aren't looking for either a hot meal or a place to stay?" he folded his arms across his chest.

She opened her mouth but closed it before she spoke a word. A lump formed in her throat, and she inhaled a deep breath as she lifted her hand, resting her palm on the handle of the gun holstered on her hip.

"I came here looking for yeh."

Mr. Carter blinked, and his head jerked again. His mouth gaped open, and he pressed his hand against his chest. "Me?" A slight chuckle vibrated through his chest. "You are looking for me?"

"Aye, I am." Her pulse deafened her ears, and her breathing shallowed. She hadn't known how she would feel at this moment, and her mind bordered on being an utter mess and being determinedly focused on the man staring at her with wide eyes.

"Why in the world are you looking for me for? Who are you?"

"Does the name Patrick McLaren mean anything to yeh?" she asked.

"Who?" Mr. Carter's brow furrowed, and he cocked his head to the side. "I'm sorry, but I don't know who that is."

While she didn't know why there was a fit of odd anger that fluttered through her chest at the notion that this man didn't have the decency to remember her pa, if he'd meant enough to Mr. Carter for Mr. Carter to think it proper to take her pa's life, then Mr. Carter should have remembered him.

"Yeh should know him. Yeh should know him well."

Mr. Carter lifted his hands, waving them. "I think you need to leave."

"I'm not leaving until I've said me peace." Her voice growled.

"Yes, you are. Get off my property."

"But this isn't yer property, is it? Yer just hiding out here because yer nothing but a criminal who is running from the Pinkertons."

His eyes narrowed, and he pointed a finger at her. "Is that who you are? Are you a Pinkerton?"

"No."

"You need to leave my property before I make you."

"I asked yeh a question. Does the name Patrick McLaren mean anything to yeh?"

"No, it doesn't. Now, off with you before I lose my patience." He waved his hand and turned away from her.

Seeing his back turned away from her flared her anger, and she pictured how he'd done the same to her pa as her pa lay on the ground, gasping for breath and bleeding from the gunshot in his chest.

She grabbed the gun holstered at her hip, drew it, and as she pointed the end of the barrel at Mr. Carter, she cocked it.

The click made him halt, but he didn't turn around.

"Patrick McLaren was my pa," she shouted at Mr. Carter. She waited, pausing as she watched him turn back toward her.

His eyes narrowed. "So?"

"Yeh shot him at the fair in Missouri about ten years ago. I was watching from behind some crates while yeh argued with him over the money yeh owed him. After yeh shot him, yeh just left him to die."

"That wasn't me."

"Of course, it was yeh!" Her raised shouts hissed through her clenched teeth. "I've never forgotten yer face or the sound of yer voice. Yeh took everything from me that day."

"I'm sorry, but you have the wrong man."

"No. I don't, and I know I don't. Yeh know I don't either, and denying it only makes yeh a coward. Yer wanted for other murders. Yer nothing but a criminal."

Her heart thumped, and she blinked. In that second, he reached behind his back and yanked a gun from his belt, pointing it at her.

"Then I suppose it's fine if I do away with you too," he said.

THIRTEEN

NICOLAS

*N*icolas spurred his horse down a long winding path beside the riverbank. The path weaved through tall prairie grass and into a grove of trees as it weaved and bent north. His heart thumped, and his lungs sounded like the horse's thundering breaths under him even though he wasn't running.

He didn't want to think about the chance that he could be too late and what he could find. Would he find the woman he had fallen for dead? Or would he find that she'd bested Mr. Carter, condemning herself as a wanted criminal?

No. He couldn't think about it. Not now.

He spurred his horse into a faster pace, and the horse's hooves pounded the ground.

~

*S*moke billowed through the trees in the distance, and the scent of a campfire wafted in Nicolas's nose. He headed toward the smell and, riding over a small hill, came upon the river and the cabin. He looked across the water, catching sight of Charlotte sitting on her horse and pointing a gun at a man standing mere feet from her. The man had a gun, too, pointed at her. The two locked in a standoff that nearly knocked the breath from Nicolas's lungs.

"Mr. Carter!" he shouted, hoping that by calling Mr. Carter's name, he would distract them both, not giving Mr. Carter the upper hand on Charlotte.

It worked.

Although they both glanced at him, Charlotte focused back on Mr. Carter while Mr. Carter was forced to watch them both. He stepped back a few steps, turning his head side to side, glancing between Charlotte and Nicolas.

"Is he with you?" Mr. Carter asked her.

"I wouldn't say that." Her voice bit the air. She wasn't happy to see Nicolas. Not in the slightest.

"Miss McLaren, you need to step back and let the law handle this." Nicolas cued his horse to cross the river, and as Mr. Carter struggled to decide whom to point his gun at, Nicolas drew his, pointing it at the trembling man on foot. "Don't get any ideas, Mr. Carter."

"I don't know who you are or what you're doing here, but I'm innocent, and I want you both off my property."

Nicolas shook his head, and after halting his horse next to Charlotte's, he dropped the reins onto the horse's neck and dug into his jacket pocket, yanking out a folded piece of paper. "I can't do that, Mr. Carter. I have a warrant for your arrest. We can do this the easy way, and you can come with me back to Missouri without fighting me, or we can do this the hard way, and I'll drag you back to Missouri by your feet. It's your choice."

Mr. Carter pointed toward Charlotte. "Is this because of her saying I killed her father?"

"Yeh did kill him. In an alleyway, while the fair was in town."

The louder she shouted, the more pronounced her Irish accent became.

Mr. Carter stared at her for a moment, then smiled. A thought seemed to inch through his mind, and he snorted as he jerked his head. "You can't prove it, so I didn't do it."

She cued her horse forward, still holding her gun pointed at him. "I don't have to prove anything. I know it, and that's all that matters."

"Charlotte, don't," Nicolas warned.

"Don't what? Do what I've been planning for years?"

"Go ahead." Mr. Carter snorted again and chuckled. "Do it then because I don't think you can."

"I wouldn't underestimate her, Mr. Carter," Nicolas said. Although he knew she shouldn't, nor did he want her to, he also knew the fire in her. She would pull the trigger, and she had no problem doing so. He heaved a deep sigh. "Charlotte, if you do this . . . I will have to arrest you for murder. Criminal or not, Mr. Carter is still a man, and if you kill him . . ." Nicolas let his voice trail off. Not because he knew she understood the threat he hinted toward but because he couldn't bring himself to utter it.

"I don't care about yer laws," she said. Her voice hinted between a fierce determination with just a little bit of fear. As though there was a bit of hesitation inside of her.

"Please, Charlotte, just back your horse up and let me take him."

Nicolas closed his eyes, just for a second, as he whispered a silent prayer that she would listen to him.

~

CHARLOTTE

*A*lthough she knew she should listen to the Pinkerton, she didn't want to. She'd waited years and years for this moment, and she couldn't believe he was asking her to give it up. Did he not understand what this meant for her? Did he not know she couldn't do that?

He had to be nothing but a bloody fool to think she'd just give up and walk away.

"Please, Charlotte," he said again. His voice was stern, but there was a hint of begging to the tone. "Just back your horse up and let me take him."

Charlotte bit her lip for a moment and inhaled a deep breath. "I can't do that," she said.

"Yes, you can. Just lower your weapon. Start with that."

"Yeh don't understand. I can't. And I don't want to."

"I know you don't, but you have to."

"How about this?" Mr. Carter said, interrupting them. "How about you both go and leave me be on my property?"

Both Nicolas and Charlotte looked at the man, and as he smiled, Charlotte lost the last of the patience holding her back. She shot off a round, missing Mr. Carter and hitting the dirt near his feet.

Mr. Carter jumped and shot back at her, missing her.

She jerked back on her horse, and it reared, knocking her to the ground. Her body hit the dirt with a thud.

She heard Nicolas cuss, and he jumped off his horse, firing his own gun several times at Mr. Carter, who shot back at them both.

Charlotte rolled over, pointing her gun as Mr. Carter took aim at Nicolas and shot him in the arm. Nicolas dropped his gun and grabbed the side of his arm. He bent down, reaching for the weapon as Mr. Carter aimed again.

Charlotte sucked in a breath and pulled the trigger, nailing Mr. Carter in the chest.

Mr. Carter stumbled backward a few steps as he glanced down at the wound on his own body. He dropped to his knees, furrowing his brow as he dropped his gun and looked over at her as she rose to her feet and made her way toward him. She pointed her gun at his head.

"Yeh remember my pa, don't yeh?" she asked him.

Mr. Carter closed his eyes and nodded.

"And yeh murdered him, didn't yeh?"

Mr. Carter blinked slowly. He opened his mouth but closed it without saying a word.

"Charlotte." Nicolas approached behind her, holding his arm.

She ignored him, keeping her focus on Mr. Carter. "And yeh murdered him, didn't yeh?" she asked again, raising her voice. "Didn't yeh?"

Mr. Carter closed his eyes and nodded again.

A flame of anger flared in her chest, and she pulled the trigger again.

～

NICOLAS

*N*icolas watched Mr. Carter collapse on the ground. His lifeless body lay in the dirt, and Nicolas winced as he bent down and grabbed his gun. Pain shot through his arm and up into his shoulder, and as he felt the back of his arm, he knew the bullet had gone clean through. He untied the bandana from around his leg and tucked it under his arm, using his teeth to hold one end while he tried to tie it down as a tourniquet.

"Here," Charlotte said as she knelt beside him. "Let me do that. We should get yeh back to the wagon, so I can clean it and get the bullet out."

"It went straight through."

"Well, I still need to clean it and, I guess, cauterize it." Her voice cracked a little. She tied the bandana tight around his arm.

She heaved a deep breath, and her eyes glanced from the ground and then back to his. "I suppose yeh'll have to arrest me, then, after that."

A lump formed in his throat, and as much as he wanted to swallow it, he couldn't. Duty bound him to say yes and to take her in his custody if she killed a man. His heart told him otherwise.

"I don't think I'll be doing that today," he said.

"Oh. I suppose tomorrow then, after yer feeling better?"

He furrowed his eyebrows. "Nah, I don't think it will be tomorrow either. In fact, why don't we just say that . . . that it was me who took down Mr. Carter?"

"Won't yeh get in trouble?"

"I'm the law, Charlotte. It's my job, and although they'd like to see criminals stand trial for their crimes if we must take other measures . . . well, then we do."

"Yeh would lie for me?" She cocked her head to the side, dropping her gaze to the ground before looking at him again. "Why?"

He sucked in a breath and reached out, sliding his hand up the side of her cheek. "Because I'm finding the idea of living a life without you in it hard to think about."

She stared at him for a moment, and his heart thumped with the thoughts that she didn't feel the same way he did and that what he said wasn't something she wanted to hear. He thought about her pulling away from him and how he didn't want to know how it would feel.

Instead, she leaned into him, pressing her lips against his.

"I don't want to live without yeh either," she whispered. "I didn't want yeh angry with me, but I had to do it. I couldn't walk away from him."

"I understand. I know why you did it. I told myself I would say anything to protect you if you did."

"We need to get yeh back to the wagon before yeh lose any more blood." She stood, wrapping her arm around his shoulder. "Let me help yeh back on yer horse."

∼

CHARLOTTE

*T*here was little time to talk to anyone when they reached the wagons. Instead, Charlotte went to work on Nicolas's arm, cleaning the wound before taking a knife blade to the fire to heat it. She hadn't wanted to hurt him in any way, but by the time she was finished, his whole body was slick with sweat, and his lungs heaved.

"I'm sorry. I didn't mean to hurt yeh," she whispered, tossing the hot knife blade into the bucket of water.

"I understand." He lay against the wheel of the wagon and closed his eyes. His body still trembled, and he clutched his elbow, holding his arm tight against him.

She glanced at Uncle Ned kneeling feet from her. Tears streamed down his face, and as she stood to move toward him, he rushed to her, wrapping his arms around her and squeezing tight.

"I thought I'd lost yeh," he whispered.

"I'm sorry to have worried yeh. I didn't mean to do it."

"I should be flaming, bloody mad at yeh, Lass. But I can't bring meself to do it." He pulled away and glanced at Nicolas. "Is he going to be all right?"

"I think so. I wish Sadie were here."

"Who is Sadie?" Nicolas asked. He kept one eye closed as he opened the other one.

"A very close friend." She crouched next to him, grabbing a

cloth from a different water bucket and wiping his face for what felt like the hundredth time since they got to the wagons. "And she's a doctor."

"I don't think I need a doctor." He offered a slight smile and then closed the one eye, taking a deep breath as he seemed to fall asleep.

Uncle Ned and Charlotte watched him for a moment before Uncle Ned motioned her to follow him over to the campfire.

"Care to tell me what happened?" he asked.

"Not really, but I want yeh to know it's done. Mr. Carter is dead."

Uncle Ned inhaled a deep breath through his nose as he nodded. "Aye. That's good to hear. Now yeh can finally find some peace."

"Aye. I suppose." Her gaze dropped to the ground. Although she'd thought of this day more times than she could count, there was one thing she never could imagine—how she would feel. It was something she couldn't predict, and while she knew she would feel a sense of relief, that was about the only emotion she could plan on. Everything else was a mystery, and if she were honest with herself, it still kind of was.

She didn't know how she felt at this moment.

Relieved.

Sad.

And, lastly, odd—as though she now saw the world differently, and she wondered if she still fit in it.

"What's the matter, Lass?"

She glanced at Uncle Ned and shrugged. "It's nothing."

"Don't be doing that to me now. I know when something is bothering yeh."

She opened her mouth but hesitated for a moment. "I can't picture my life without him."

"Mr. Carter?"

"No." She chuckled. "Nicolas."

"I see. And why do yeh say that as though it's a problem?"

"Because I don't know how a lady can shoot a man dead one day and then become the wife of another the next, bearing his children along the way. Don't me actions tarnish me? Don't they make me undesirable? I feel as though I've sinned so greatly; there isn't hope for me anymore."

"Have yeh spoken to him about it?"

Before she could speak, Nicolas opened his eyes and glanced up at them, answering for her. "No, she hasn't." His deep voice was hoarse and strained.

"Yeh should rest."

"I will later." He glanced over to the ground next to him. "Come sit with me for a minute."

Uncle Ned made his way toward the other wagons as she moved over to Nicolas and sat beside him.

"So, what is this nonsense I hear? That you are tarnished?"

"I shot a man."

"And I have shot many. Does that make me unable to be a good husband?"

"No. But yer a man. It's different."

"Only if someone wants to see it that way. And I don't." He chuckled, wincing through his laugh, but laughing anyway. "I kind of see it as a good quality. At least I don't have to worry about my wife being unable to protect herself or our children."

Her stomach fluttered, and her cheeks flushed with warmth. "So, is that proposal then?" she asked.

He smiled, snorting as he jerked his head back. "Yeah. I guess it is. If you don't mind marrying a gruff and stubborn Pinkerton."

"I think I can manage that kind of man."

"I love your confidence."

She leaned over, kissing him. "And I love yers."

"There's a reverend on the wagon train, right?" he asked.

She smiled and nodded. "How soon are yeh looking for us to get hitched?"

He cocked his head to the side, closing one eye as he glanced around the sky. "It sure is a pretty afternoon. It looks like it will be a pretty night too. I think it would be perfect for a wedding. Don't you think?"

She laughed. "Let me go find the reverend."

SIX MONTHS LATER

CHARLOTTE

harlotte trotted across the road toward the Grand Hotel. She knew she was early, but she couldn't help it. Far too excited to sit at home for another minute, she'd rushed into town, holding onto her growing belly as she hurried. She didn't want to think about all the people staring at a pregnant woman running across the road, mostly because she didn't care.

She darted up the stairs and crossed the porch, opening the door with a force that nearly sent the wood into the frame behind it. She was looking for only one face, and it didn't take long for her to find it.

"We were wondering when you would arrive," a voice said from the parlor room.

Charlotte smiled as she turned toward the parlor, and Sadie stood from one of the chairs, a smile beaming across her face.

"You're late," she said.

"And here I thought I was early." Charlotte cocked her head to the side, moving toward her friend as Emma, Abby, and Lillian all stood from their seats, and all five women embraced in tight hugs.

Emma bounced on her toes. "We're all back together again." Her infant son, Joseph, squirmed in her arms, and she adjusted his blanket around him. "I'm sorry," she said to him. The spitting image of James, he'd been the first of the babies from the wagon train born in Oregon.

"And this time, it's for good," Sadie said.

"What do you mean?" Abby asked, cuddling with her daughter, Meredith, who followed Joseph not long after.

"Well, I was waiting for Charlotte to arrive, but the reason I sent you all a letter and asked you to meet me here was to tell you that Charles and I are moving to Portland. He's opening up a practice, and my father is staying in Swallow Creek."

"So, we'll all be together again?" Abby gasped, looking between the other women.

While James and Emma and Abby and William had found houses at the other edge of town, the two, along with Lillian and Everett, stayed close to Charlotte and Nicolas, allowing the four to host dinners and parties with the rest.

The only two who had been missing were Sadie and Charles.

"Well, this is just the best news," Lillian said. "We've all missed you so much."

"And I have missed you all too. I'm so excited that our children will all know each other." Sadie looked down at her adopted son, Matthew, while he sat and played on the floor with Marie, Lillian and Everett's daughter. She turned to Charlotte. "What do you think about it?"

"It's a dream come true." Charlotte hugged her friend.

"Who would have thought when we left Missouri all those months ago that we would all find love and happiness?" Sadie asked.

Emma lifted her finger, wiggling it at the other women. "Don't forget family. We found family too."

Charlotte smiled at each woman she'd come to know and love like sisters. "Aye, we certainly did at that."

THE END

DID YOU READ THEM ALL?

Five women on the trip of their lives . . .

Five men who stumble across their paths . . .

One wagon train where they all will either live happily ever after or leave with shattered dreams.

CHECK OUT THE SERIES ON AMAZON! AND PICK UP THE ONES YOU MAY HAVE MISSED TODAY!

OREGON TRAIL BRIDES

Four orphans and their headmistress set out for Oregon in search of men looking for mail-order brides. Will they find what they are looking for? Or will fate have other plans?

SERIES RELEASES STARTING IN APRIL 2023

JOIN MY MAILING LIST TO KEEP UP-TO-DATE ON THE RELEASE OF THE OREGON TRAIL BRIDES SERIES!

BRIDES OF LONE HOLLOW

Five men looking for love . . .

Five women with different ideas . . .

One small town where they all will either live happily ever after or
leave with shattered dreams.

TURN THE PAGE FOR A SNEAK PEEK AT BOOK ONE, HER MAIL ORDER
MIX-UP.

ONE

CULLEN

"God never gives you what He can't carry you through."

Pastor Duncan's words repeated in Cullen McCray's mind as he glanced down at his niece. All of just nine years old, the little girl sat beside him in the wagon as they drove into town. Her little body bumped into his every time a wheel rolled over a rock, and her white-blonde hair blew in the gentle breeze. She was the purest example of what the pastor was talking about. Or at least that was what the pastor had told him when he brought her to Cullen's cabin that day, scared and sad. Her entire world was torn apart by her father's sudden death and him, her uncle, her only chance.

She glanced back at him. Her eyes---his brother's eyes---stared at him. She looked more like Clint every day, and he wondered if she would grow up to have Clint's mannerisms. Would she act like him? Talk like him? Would she think like him? While he wanted her to, a part of him didn't. He wasn't sure he wanted another Clint in his life.

"What do we need from town today, Uncle Cullen?" Sadie asked.

He rolled the piece of straw from one side of his lips to the other, chewing a little more on the sweet taste of the dried stem. "Just the usual, Sadie. Did you need something else this time?"

She shrugged. "I was thinking of making a pie when we got back to the ranch."

Pie.

He hadn't thought of pie in months, hadn't thought about much of the things his late wife used to bake, actually. Because thinking of them would have reminded him of her and how she wasn't around to bake them anymore. He ate chili and stew and steak and potatoes and eggs and bacon, which was the sum of his diet. Perhaps he would have some bread or biscuits on those cold winter nights when he needed something to stick to the sides of his gut and keep him warm, but other than that, he didn't branch out. He didn't want to. He didn't want the reminder.

Of course, he knew that needed to change now that Sadie was in his life. He had to care for her, and a little growing girl needed more nourishment than what he'd been putting into his body. She needed a garden with lots of vegetables and an orchard with fruit trees. She needed bread. She needed cakes and cookies and, well, pie. All the things his late wife would spend her days making for him. He could still smell all the scents in the house. But back to the point. Sadie needed more, and she also needed to cook and bake—or at least learn to do those things along with how to sew, read, and do arithmetic.

"Do you know how to bake a pie?" he asked the girl.

"I do. Well, sort of. It was one thing Nanny Noreen taught me before . . ." The little girl's voice trailed off. She didn't want to say before the accident. She never did. She always stopped herself when she found the words trying to come out of her lips.

Not that he blamed her. He never wished to speak of it, either. His brother and his sister-in-law were now up in Heaven with his wife, leaving Sadie and him down here on earth to pick up the pieces as best as they could.

"What kind of pie did you want to make?" he asked; a slight hope rose in his chest that the girl would say peach or apple. Those were always his favorite.

"I don't know. I guess whatever fruit I can find in town."

Find in town.

Guilt prickled in his chest. She shouldn't have to find fruit in town. She should be able to go out and pick it off her tree. It was just another thing he mentally put on his list of things to do for her—plant some trees.

"Well, I suppose we can look to see what Mr. Dawson has. If you find something that works, we can get it. Did you need anything else for a pie?"

"I don't know. I suppose if I may, I'll look around?"

"Yeah. You can do that."

She glanced at him again and smiled before leaning her head on his arm.

His heart gave another little tug at his guilt. For so many months after the accident and after Pastor Duncan brought her up to his cabin, he hadn't wanted her to stay. Not quite a burden, but almost there. He had packed her bags, he didn't know how many times, fully intent on taking her down to the orphanage where he thought she belonged. She needed a chance at a family with a ma and pa. She didn't need a gruff lone wolf like him. Not to mention, he had wished to live his life alone in his cabin. The cattle ranch. The family. Those were all things Clint, his brother, wanted. He didn't. Or at least he didn't until . . .

He shook his head, ridding himself of the thoughts of his late wife.

He couldn't think of her.

Not now.

Not today.

Never again.

He tapped the reins on the horses' backs, then whistled at them to pick up the pace into a trot. He needed the distraction of town to ease his mind.

~

MAGGIE

"*L*ove always, Clint." Maggie once again read the ending words of Clint's last letter as the stagecoach rolled down the lane. Her heart thumped, and she bit her lip as she leaned back in the seat and rested her head back.

She didn't want to think about the life she left to travel hundreds of miles across the United States so she could marry a man she didn't know. Or how she fled her parents' house in the middle of the night with her mother telling her to leave while her father slept. She only wanted to think about the life she was about to start as Mrs. Clint McCray. It didn't matter that they hadn't actually met before and had only corresponded with letters. Nor did it matter that she wasn't exactly in love with him . . . yet. It only mattered that in those letters, he promised her a life far away from her parents and the life they had planned for her. One where Daddy would shove her into a loveless marriage with either Benjamin Stone or Matthew Cooper— two sons of business acquaintances he'd known for years. She knew both men well, too. Benjamin was nothing but a bore, and Matthew . . . well, let her just say she didn't care for the way he treated women. Not to mention, his reputation in town left little to be desired, and she doubted the perpetual bachelor would even want to marry. He had more fun pursuing other tastes.

While she knew her daddy didn't think they were the best choices, he also wasn't about to have a spinster for a daughter, and she knew her time was fast ticking away. As did her mama. Which was why, when Clint's letter arrived with the plan for her to leave, they packed her a suitcase and bought her a ticket out west. Out to Lone Hollow, Montana.

"Are you headed to Lone Hollow?" the woman sitting across from her asked. Slightly older than Maggie, her hair was styled in a tight bun at the base of her neck, and she looked through a pair of spectacles resting on her long, thin nose.

"Yes, I am. My soon-to-be husband lives there and is waiting for me."

The woman smiled and ducked her chin slightly. "Best wishes to you both."

"Thank you. I'm Maggie, by the way. Maggie Colton."

The woman nodded. "Amelia Hawthorn. It's a pleasure to meet you."

"You, too." Maggie shifted her gaze from the woman to the window of the stagecoach. Nothing but mountains and forests and wilderness, Montana had been nothing like she'd ever seen before. So pretty. So peaceful. Like God's perfect place and glory was here in this state. "Where are you headed?" she asked, turning her attention to the woman.

"Brook Creek. It's about forty miles west of Lone Hollow."

"So, you still have a bit to go in your travels."

"Unfortunately. But I figure I've been this far. As long as I get to my post, I don't mind the distance."

"Post?"

"I'm a schoolteacher, and I received my post orders for the small town. I had asked for Lone Hollow, seeing as how it's a milling town, but was told it was filled . . . at least for now."

"A milling town? Does that make it a more appealing post?"

"A little. Lone Hollow has one of the few sawmills around,

and having a sawmill means more amenities than Brook Creek, like a hotel and café. There is more of a population in Lone Hollow than in Brook Creek, too, which means there are more families and children. They told me they would tell me if the teacher in Lone Hollow leaves, and if he does, then I will move again as I'm not sure I want to stay in Brook Creek."

The name made Maggie giggle. "It's funny that the town is named for two synonyms for a river."

"Don't get me started on that." The woman rolled her eyes and exhaled a deep sigh as she slid her fingers behind her ears, tucking any loose strands of her blonde bun behind her ears. The feathers on her maroon hat fluttered with her movement, and they matched her maroon dress. "Of course, all I care about are the children. I hope they are nice and are ready to learn."

"I'm sure they are, and you will do fine." Maggie bit her lip again at the thoughts in her head. She dropped her gaze to her hands, fidgeting with her fingers. "My husband-to-be has a daughter. She is nine years old. His first wife died of Scarlet Fever several years ago when she was just a baby. I feel awful that she was never able to meet her mother."

"Such a shame she lost her mama."

"Yes, it is. I just hope I can bond with her. I don't wish to replace her mother, but I hope to be someone she can accept and love."

"I'm sure she will. It might take some time, but you will do just fine."

Maggie glanced at the woman and smiled as she nodded. She didn't know if she could talk anymore about the young girl or her concerns, for the notions brought more butterflies to her stomach than the thoughts of meeting Clint. She wanted to do right by the young girl and wanted to be someone the girl could trust, look up to, and perhaps love after time had passed. She knew how wonderful it was to grow up with a mother, and she wanted that for Sadie.

The stagecoach slowed, and with the change of pace, Maggie glanced out the window again. While the mountains and forests were still in her view, a few houses speckled what little she could see, and as more and more passed by, the stagecoach slowed as it finally entered the town of Lone Hollow.

TWO

CULLEN

ullen halted the horses in front of the general store, and as Sadie climbed from the wagon and trotted inside, he jumped down himself and tied the reins to the tie post. The morning sun shone down on the back of his neck, causing a thin layer of sweat that he wiped away after yanking the handkerchief from his back pocket. He made a mental note of the things he needed—sugar, flour, more seeds for their new garden, and some much-needed equipment to help him with the tasks. How Clint had tended to the old garden they had at the ranch in past years with the broken and rusted tools in the barn, he didn't know.

He also didn't want to forget he needed nails for the lumber he picked up from the sawmill the other day. The old barn had a wall that needed fixing before winter set in, or else he didn't think it would withstand another few months of the wind, ice, and snow.

Actually, the whole thing needed fixing—or to be replaced—but he wanted to at least take it one wall at a time.

"Good morning, Mr. McCray." Mr. Dawson smiled as Cullen

entered the store. His voice boomed over the bell that chimed as the door opened the closed.

"Morning."

"I saw Sadie run past a few minutes ago. She darted over in the corner as though she was determined to find something." The owner slightly chuckled as he adjusted his glasses up his nose.

"She's fixing to make a pie this afternoon."

"Oh? A pie. Sounds delicious. I have some nice apples that Mr. Smith brought in yesterday from his orchard. I tried one myself, and they are bright red on the outside and juicy on the inside. They should make some lovely pies."

"Well, then I suppose I see an apple pie in my future for dinner, then."

The two men chuckled at Cullen's joke as Cullen leaned against the counter.

"So, what can I do for you today?" Mr. Dawson asked.

"Just the usual. Plus, I need a new rake, hoe, and shovel. I'm going to expand the garden at the ranch this spring. Let Sadie have fun growing what we will eat in the winter."

"Sounds like she'll enjoy that."

Cullen ducked his chin for a moment, lowering his voice. "I sure hope so."

Mr. Dawson laid his hand on Cullen's shoulder. "Mrs. Dawson and I were talking about what happened to your brother and how you've taken the girl in and cared for her. You're doing a mighty fine thing, Mr. McCray, and a mighty fine job, too. The whole town thinks so. You shouldn't doubt yourself."

Cullen nodded. "Thank you. I'm trying. Sometimes I do not know why God gave a guy like me a girl to raise."

"Because He knows what He's doing."

The door opened, and the bell above it chimed again. Cullen glanced over, meeting Pastor Duncan's gaze as he strolled in.

The pastor nodded and tipped his hat to the two men before taking it off and tossing it on the counter.

"Morning, gentlemen," he said.

"Morning, Pastor." While Mr. Dawson returned the salutation, Cullen only nodded. An air of being uncomfortable squared in his chest. He hadn't seen the pastor in a while, and the last time he did was when the pastor brought Sadie up to his cabin with the news . . . and well, he hadn't been pleasant to the old man. In fact, he'd been downright rude, and while at the time he thought he was justified, there were times he felt he'd overreacted.

Pastor Duncan nodded back to the store owner and yanked a slip of paper from his pocket. "Mr. Dawson, I have some special requests I need to make this morning, and I'm hoping you don't have to order any of them."

"Sure thing." Mr. Dawson held out his hand. "Give me the order. I'll see what I can do after I get Mr. McCray loaded."

"Oh, there's no need for that. Just bring what you have for me out here. I'll load it myself," Cullen said, hoping the gesture would make up—even if it were just a little—for the past.

"Are you sure?"

"Yes, I'm sure. See to the Pastor's order. I'm in no hurry."

As Mr. Dawson vanished in the store's backroom, Pastor Duncan leaned against the counter. He glanced at Cullen a few times before clearing his throat. "Did you bring Miss Sadie with you?"

"She's over there, gathering things to make a pie this afternoon."

"A pie?" The pastor's eyebrows raised as he smiled. "Sounds like you will have a splendid dinner this evening."

"If she doesn't burn the house down." Cullen chuckled to himself a bit.

"It also sounds like she's doing all right. After . . . everything."

"She seems to be. She has her moments as I would expect anyone to have, having been through what she's been through."

"And how are you handling everything?"

"All right, too, I suppose." He paused for a moment, clearing his throat. "Listen, Pastor, about the last time we spoke—"

"There's nothing to say about that."

"But there is. I wasn't . . . I was rude to you, and I shouldn't have been. I can't imagine it was easy for you, bringing Sadie to my cabin with the news."

"It wasn't that bad. I figure since it was His plan, I might as well help Him orchestrate it." The pastor smiled. "We haven't seen you around church lately. I was hoping you would start coming again now that you have Sadie."

A flicker of guilt prickled in Cullen's chest. He knew how wrong it was to skip church every week. But it had been the one thing he and his wife shared, had been their favorite time together, and since her death, he hadn't been able to even think about setting foot inside that place. Every inch screamed her. Every wooden pew. Every window. The door. The pulpit. Even the floor that she'd walked down dressed in a white dress to become his wife.

Now she lay in the ground in the small graveyard next to it.

That was another reason he hadn't been back. He hadn't visited her grave since the funeral.

"I'll think about next Sunday, and I'll ask Sadie if she wants to go," he lied.

Pastor Duncan's eyes narrowed for a moment before they softened. "Children rarely know what's best for them, and it's up to their parents to tell them what they need to learn and do."

"Yeah, well, I'm not her parent."

"You are. It's just a different kind of parent."

Cullen opened his mouth to argue again but stopped himself as the little girl bounded around one of the shelves. A broad grin etched across her face as she held an armful of bright red apples.

"Uncle Cullen! Uncle Cullen! Mr. Dawson has apples. Lots of red and juicy-looking apples. I think I'll try to make an apple pie, maybe even two pies. What do you think?"

"I think it sounds delicious, Sadie."

Her smile widened even more, and she handed him every one, she carried.

"Hello, Pastor Duncan," she said, noticing him standing there.

"Good morning, Sadie. How are you this fine morning?"

"Good." A memory seemed to flicker in her mind, and her face twisted a little. Her smile faded. While Cullen wasn't sure of the thoughts suddenly weighing on her mind, he could guess that it had to do with the fact that the last time she'd seen the pastor was when he brought her to Cullen's cabin to let Cullen know, not only of his brother's death but that Sadie was now in his custody. He didn't want to imagine what that time had been like for her. Having lived through both her parents' deaths, she was now an orphan and coming to live with a man she only knew a little.

As Cullen put the apples on the counter, Mr. Dawson returned from the back with his arms full. "I was able to gather most of what you needed, Pastor Duncan," he said, setting it all down.

"It's a sign from God, then. It's going to be a great day."

Cullen stepped away from the counter as the pastor and store owner finished their transaction. A small part of him hoped the subject of church wouldn't come up again, at least not in front of Sadie, before he had a chance to talk to her. He didn't know if he wanted even to mention it, at least not until he was ready—which he was far from it—and he didn't need the pressure of being roped into it before then.

The pastor said nothing, however, and after paying for his

supplies, he tipped his hat to them, gave Sadie an extra wave and a smile, and left the store without another word.

Cullen breathed a sigh of relief as he laid his hand on Sadie's shoulder and guided her around the counter. "Let's help Mr. Dawson get our supplies from the back and then get them loaded into our wagon."

~

MAGGIE

The stagecoach came to a complete stop in front of the Lone Hollow Hotel, and Maggie climbed out. Her boots touched down on the dirt road, and she lifted her hand to shield her eyes from the sun. It helped a little, but she still had to squint as she glanced from one direction to the other. Clint had said he would wait for her at the hotel, but no one had even approached her as the driver handed over her luggage. Shrugging off the slight air of confusion, she crossed the hotel's porch and sat down on a bench just outside the door. The wood planks showed little kindness to her shoes as the humid moisture in the air stuck to her skin. The sun's heat deepened, weighing on her with a heavy thickness.

Perhaps he got tied up or something and is just running late, she thought.

As the stagecoach's driver finished unloading a few parcels that were obviously en route to people who lived in the town, he climbed back into his seat and cued the horses down the road. Maggie could see Amelia wave just before the carriage vanished around the corner, and she couldn't help but smile when she thought of the small town of Brook Creek.

Who names these towns, anyway, she thought.

People meandered through the streets while Maggie continued to wait on the bench under the overhang, and she glanced around at the hotel to keep her mind busy. It wasn't the worst one she'd ever seen, but it wasn't the best either, looking as though years of weathered seasons had taken a toll on the old wood—the once bright shade of dark red paint had faded into a pale cherry color.

"Top of the mornin' to yeh, Miss," called a voice from the building across the street. She jerked her head around to find a short, plump man tipping his hat to a woman walking toward him. The woman smiled and waved as she passed, and he watched her for a moment before returning to the sweeping he had been doing on the porch in front of a building that looked like a café. The volume of his thick Irish accent overwhelmed the chirping birds in the oak trees above, and he turned his body slightly as a pair of young boys ran past him, one betting the other he could leap up and batter the painted sign while the other could not. However, upon catching the man's glare, they both seemed to realize their theory would go unproven.

More people meandered along the storefront while a man tossed supplies into the back of a wagon while a little girl watched. Her white-blonde curls bounced from not only her movement but the gentle breeze in the air.

Maggie checked her pocket watch. The stagecoach hadn't been early or late, but right on time, and a flicker of concern rested in her stomach. She had gotten the correct date, hadn't she? She reached into her handbag and yanked out the letter, unfolding it as she read it one more time.

"You should arrive on the 10th of April by wagon. I will wait for you." She read the words of Clint's letter in a whisper to herself.

Today was the 10th of April, was it not? She was certain it was.

"Good morning, Miss," a voice said.

She glanced up. Her heart thumped.

"Are you new in town?" The older gentleman said. He tipped his hat before taking it off. "My name is Pastor John Duncan."

She let out a deep breath and stood. "Miss Maggie Colton."

"Sorry for the intrusion. I just saw you sitting here, and it looked as though you were waiting for someone."

"I am. Mr. Clint McCray. I'm his . . . wife-to-be, I suppose you could say. We've been corresponding for several months, and he sent for me so we can be married." She showed him the envelope and piece of paper she was reading as though she thought it would prove her story. Not that she thought the pastor didn't believe her, it just seemed like the thing to do.

He didn't take it, and instead, he jerked his head and blinked as though shocked.

Her stomach twisted. What had she said that seemed wrong? Perhaps she should give a little more detail, hoping to gain some insight into what the pastor was thinking. "He said he would wait for me when I arrived. See? It's all here in this letter. Do you know him?"

"Well, yes, I do . . . but . . ." The pastor glanced over his shoulder, hooking his thumb. He paused for a moment as though watching someone, then turned back to her. "Actually, Mr. McCray is just over there, loading supplies into his wagon."

She had noticed the man earlier. Perhaps he had wanted to get everything loaded before he came for her. "Ah, yes, that man with his daughter. I see. Her name is Sadie, correct?"

"That would be them—Mr. McCray and Sadie McCray." Pastor Duncan moved, stepping aside and motioning her toward the road as if to give her permission to cross it so she could finally be with the one she'd been waiting on. "It was a pleasure meeting you, Miss Colton."

"The pleasure is all mine." She shook his hand again, then bent down, grabbing her suitcases before she looked in both directions and trekked across the road.

Her heart thumped with each step, and as she neared Clint,

she blew out a breath. This was it. This was their moment. The one she could picture in her mind. He would smile. She would smile. They would hug and tell each other how happy they were to meet each other finally. He was more handsome than she had even thought. With broad shoulders and this rough exterior with chocolate hair, a subtle beard, and arms that as they tossed bags of supplies in the wagon, she imagined them wrapped around her. Her excitement fluttered in her chest, and she had to remind herself to walk, not run, to him.

"Mr. McCray?" she called out, and as Clint turned to face her, she dropped her bags and threw her arms out, wrapping them around his neck. Perhaps it wasn't exactly proper of her, but she couldn't help herself, not to mention she didn't care. "I can't believe we are finally meeting."

Clint wiggled from her grasp and backed away from her. His eyes grew wide, and his mouth gaped for a moment. "Who are you?" he asked.

"What do you mean, who am I? I'm Maggie, Maggie Colton. Your soon-to-be wife. You sent for me, and you were supposed to meet me. Remember? It's the 10th of April." Her stomach twisted with each of her words, and with each passing second that the words didn't seem to bring any clarity to him. She still had his letter in her hand, and she outstretched it. "You wrote me, telling me to come so that you and I would be married."

ORDER THE SERIES TODAY OR READ FOR **FREE** WITH KINDLE UNLIMITED

To my sister
Michelle Renee Horning

April 3, 1971 - January 8, 2022
You will be forever missed. I don't know how I'm going to do this thing
called life without you.

LONDON JAMES IS A PEN NAME FOR ANGELA CHRISTINA ARCHER. SHE LIVES ON A RANCH WITH HER HUSBAND, TWO DAUGHTERS, AND MANY FARM ANIMALS. SHE WAS BORN AND RAISED IN NEVADA AND GREW UP RIDING AND SHOWING HORSES. WHILE SHE DOESN'T SHOW ANYMORE, SHE STILL LOVES TO TRAIL RIDE.

FROM A YOUNG AGE, SHE ALWAYS WANTED TO WRITE A NOVEL. HOWEVER, EVERY TIME THE DESIRE FLICKERED, SHE SHOVED THE THOUGHT FROM MY MIND UNTIL ONE MORNING IN 2009, SHE AWOKE WITH THE DETERMINATION TO FOLLOW HER DREAM.

WWW.AUTHORLONDONJAMES.COM

JOIN MY MAILING LIST FOR NEWS ON RELEASES, DISCOUNTED SALES, AND EXCLUSIVE MEMBER-ONLY BENEFITS!

Made in the USA
Monee, IL
01 February 2024

52724563R00080